# BELLE ROUGE

by

Joyce Farmer Trammell

Vabella Publishing
P.O. Box 1052
Carrollton, Georgia 30112
*www.vabella.com*



Cover photo by Julianna Witherington.
Author's photo by Emily Maier, Emily Ray Photography.

Manufactured in the United States of America

13-digit ISBN 978-1-938230-73-8

Library of Congress Control Number 2014919976

10 9 8 7 6 5 4 3 2 1

*To Anyone who has ever faced fear and conquered it*

# PROLOGUE

Old houses have always held a curiosity for me. Who lived there? What happened to them? I've been able to get into some of the houses and I've come out of some, quite quickly. For me, it's as if they still hold the energy from their past. And some of that energy is not very pleasant.

When setting out to write a book, it isn't difficult to latch onto a story--it's more difficult to weed out those you don't want to write. It's as if many people who have passed on are clamoring to have their stories told, even though only bits and pieces of the truth are there in historical fiction.

I had begun to feel the nudge to write a book, and one house held a real fascination. I had been there twice before. Some friends, who were the relatives of the elderly man who lived there, took me along when they visited. I recognized his name as being from a prominent family who raced horses. All I remember of that day is seeing him sitting on his back porch as we drove up. After he passed away, my friends took me there to the estate sale.

As we walked toward the barn, I could see their training track behind it. I bought a horse blanket and brought it home, to my mother's dismay. I still don't know when or how she disposed of it, but the image of the house and land stayed with me. This was the place that became Belle Rouge.

# CHAPTER 1

Laurel Mackenzie turned off the main road onto a gravel driveway and maneuvered her car between the weatherbeaten stone gateposts at the farm's entrance. She was unable to see what lay ahead, for the entire length of the driveway was canopied by magnificent crimson maples. She inched the car forward eagerly trying to catch a glimpse of the mansion known as Belle Rouge. When she had first asked about the property, the real estate agent warned her. "A house that's over a hundred fifty years old is bound to have some 'stories' circulating about it."

"What kind of stories?" she remembered asking.

"You know---stories about sounds, happenings."

"Are you trying to say Belle Rouge is haunted?"

"Really, Miss MacKenzie, you don't want this house. There are plenty of others, more modern, I can show you."

The agent's words only piqued her curiosity. She had asked him for directions and insisted on going alone.

Now, as the car moved up the drive, Laurel's pulse quickened. Finally, the trees parted and the mansion came into full view. At that moment, Laurel MacKenzie knew she had to own Belle Rouge.

Certainly no ghosts had manifested themselves in the first few weeks she lived at the farm. In fact, she already felt at home in the comfortable old house. And she was thankful to be experiencing a little nudging to sit down at her typewriter, for it had been over a year since she had been able to write. Her first three novels had met with great success, but she had begun to wonder if the well of her creativity had run dry. Perhaps some of the problem was due to her restlessness. During the past year she had had an overwhelming desire to leave her home in North Carolina.

"I can't move," she argued with herself. "I've lived here all my life."

"But," another voice presented itself, "maybe it would be good to get away and start over again."

Her divorce from Robert Bradford was final and even though she had initiated the separation, she didn't like seeing him every time she went into town. She never knew what to say to him.

"Where could I go?" she asked herself. Then her mind flashed to a faded photograph she kept in a desk drawer. In the picture, an obviously happy young couple stood next to a storefront. On the window of the store were printed the words, Cedarville Hardware, R. Price, Proprietor. On the back of the photograph in her mother's handwriting were the names, Richard and Dora Price, my grandparents in Cedarville, Kentucky.

"Not a very logical way to pick a place to move," Laurel told herself. "But why not? Maybe it would be fun to find my roots."

Laurel considered herself lucky. She found it necessary to spend only a small portion of the inheritance from her parents' estate to buy Belle Rouge. She cashed in some certificates of deposit, in which she had invested with the money from her writing and opened a checking account in a local bank. She needed some cash on hand for the minor repair work on the plumbing and the electrical wiring in the mansion.

She moved to the farm in early September, just when the crimson maples were beginning to show the first hint of autumn. The furniture arrived at the designated time, and all of the antiques she had collected over the years seemed to find their niche in her new residence.

In her desire to own Belle Rouge, she had not noticed how much the weather had taken its toll on the outside trim of the stately brick house. The paint was flaking off the frame of the entrance and the large cathedral-style window. The mansion's somewhat Italianate architecture was unique, and she felt a driving force to restore it to its original beauty.

There was one thing that bothered Laurel about the house. She felt an unexplained queasiness in the pit of her stomach each time she looked up at the glass-enclosed room on top of the two-story mansion. "I know that's where the overseer stood to watch the slaves as they worked. Maybe that explains why it affects me as it does," she reasoned.

Laurel adjusted readily to life in the country, except for the time she decided to pull the weeds that had grown up around a fireplace standing some thirty feet away from the back of the house. Just as she reached down, something slid through her hand. When she drew back, a garden snake slithered between her feet.

"I don't want to tear this chimney down. I'm sure it's the only thing left when the original kitchen burned."

"Now what made me say that?" she asked herself. "I don't know that the kitchen burned. Oh, well, maybe I'll come up with something to do with the fireplace. It's an eyesore like it is."

Laurel had been settled in at Belle Rouge for a month when a phone call came. "Miss Mackenzie?" the pleasant voice inquired. "My name is Eva Farnsworth and I'm president of the Cedarville Historical Society. I was wondering if you would consider attending our meeting next Friday. I thought you might speak to us on how you go about researching your novels."

"I just write fiction, Mrs. Farnsworth."

"I know, but your historical facts are so accurate. I realize this is short notice, but we would certainly consider it a privilege if you'd speak to us."

"Well, I am about to start a new novel, and I think it will be about this area. Perhaps your historical society would have some information I could use."

"Oh, we've done extensive research on our town's history," Eva Farnsworth replied excitedly. "You can have access to anything we have."

During the days that followed, Laurel outlined her talk. It felt good to be sitting at the typewriter again. In fact, she took time to type the title page of her new novel. *The Secrets of Cedarville, by Laurel Mackenzie.*

On the evening of her scheduled talk, she rinsed the dishes, placed them in the dishwasher and found herself staring out the window at the fields, which were ragged with their uneven growth of grass. "I hate to spend more money, but I'm going to have to invest in a tractor and bush hog sooner or later," she told herself. She glanced at her watch. Eva Farnsworth was due any minute. The dilemma of the fields would have to be decided tomorrow.

Laurel waited in the parlor until she saw the headlights of a vehicle coming up the drive. The car circled in front of the house and stopped by the door. When Laurel opened it in response to the knock, she found a rather plump, gray haired woman with a ready smile standing in front of her.

"Hello, I'm Eva," came the same cheery voice she'd heard on the phone.

"Come in," Laurel returned the smile.

"Oh my, Miss Mackenzie, you've done wonders with this place. It almost looks like it did when I was a child."

"You lived at Belle Rouge?"

"No. Goodness no, but I've lived in Cedarville all my life. My family came with some of the first settlers."

"Do you know anything about the history of Belle Rouge?" Laurel asked.

"A few things," Eva replied. "My great-grandfather wrote quite a bit about the Kilgores of Belle Rouge in his record book. They were an interesting family."

"Would you mind if I read his record book---sometime when it's convenient for you?"

Eva's eyes widened. "Miss MacKenzie, is Belle Rouge going to be the setting for your next novel?"

"I think it very well might be."

Laurel climbed in the seat next to Eva Farnsworth and as the old station wagon lumbered its way down the drive, Laurel suddenly realized she was experiencing something at which she truly marveled. She felt as if Eva Farnsworth was an old, old friend. How happy she was to have found her!

About a dozen members of the historical society had gathered at the library for the monthly meeting. Laurel found all the people to be friendly and appreciative, with the exception of one man who seemed to prefer to stand alone in the back of the room. His stare was mildly disconcerting, but she completed her talk and answered questions without showing any irritation at his odd behavior.

When the audience finally moved toward the refreshment table, Eva edged her way to where Laurel stood. "Don't let Lucien bother you," she said.

"I thought I was hiding my annoyance."

"You are. It's just me," Eva's eyes twinkled. "I sometimes pick up what people are thinking."

"Are you psychic?"

"Don't say it too loudly. There are a couple of people here who would stay up all night and pray for me if they heard that word."

"Well---who's the man with the riveting eyes?" Laurel asked.

"Lucien Caulder. He only comes to the meetings once in a while. He perked up, though, when he heard you were going to speak."

Laurel accepted a cup of coffee and took a sip. "I wouldn't picture him as one of my readers."

"I don't know why not. Anyone who loves history would love your books. I've often wondered why someone doesn't make them into movies."

"My agent says we have a nibble on one," Laurel smiled.

"Oh, that's wonderful! And just to think you're living here in Cedarville now."

"Please don't spread that around. I came here where it's quiet so I could write without distraction. The fewer people who know, the better."

"I understand. But, may I please tell just one other person? That's her serving the cake. You'll like Jane. She's a very serious person, but lots of fun when you get to know her."

Laurel studied the woman standing behind the table. She was attractive, fashionably dressed and her blonde hair was done to perfection.

"Jane and I went to high school together."

"You and she?" Laurel spoke without thinking.

"Hard to believe she's sixty, isn't it?"

"Yes, it is," Laurel sighed. "I look older than she does and I'm forty."

"Come on, I want to introduce you. You'll like her."

The woman looked up as Eva and Laurel approached. "I enjoyed your talk, Miss Mackenzie," she said.

"Laurel, this is Jane Miller."

"I'm glad to meet you. Eva says I'm going to like you."

"Not everyone does," Jane winked. "I have too many ex-students still living here in Cedarville."

"Oh don't listen to her," Eva scolded. "They all loved her."

"You're a teacher?" Laurel asked.

"I used to be, but thirty years is enough. It was time to do something else."

"And what do you do now?"

Jane Miller laughed. "Sometimes Eva and I get into trouble. We travel together and work with the historical society. And we've both just finished our family genealogies."

"You've lived in Cedarville all your life, too?"

"Yes. My family came about the same time as Eva's. I could never leave here."

"I know what you mean," Laurel replied. "My attachments were pretty deep in North Carolina, but my parents are gone now. Do both of you still have relatives living here?"

"My parents are gone, too, and I never married," Jane responded. "I do have one cousin. He's a deputy sheriff."

"The only thing I have is an ex-husband," Eva giggled. "And he moved to Florida with a new thirty-year-old wife. What about you, Laurel?"

"One daughter in college. But she prefers her father's company to mine."

"Then you're divorced, too," Eva said. "Well then, how about joining forces with two old women? The three of us could probably find some kind of monkey business to get into."

"I think I'd like that. However, writing is going to take up a lot of my time, as will taking care of Belle Rouge. But I can't work all the time, and you two sound like a lot of fun."

"Good, it's settled," Eva clapped her hands. "This weekend is Cedarville's homecoming, and we could go to the sale barn on Saturday and visit all the booths."

Laurel winced. "I'm not sure I'd enjoy that."

"What better way to get acquainted with the citizens of Cedarville than to look at their junk?" Jane smiled.

"OK, why not? Would you like to meet at Belle Rouge? I'll fix breakfast."

"That sounds wonderful," Eva exclaimed. "Jane, I can't wait for you to see what Laurel's done with the house."

"I'd love to see it. But, Laurel, I've been dying to ask you a question all night. Why in the world did you move to Cedarville, of all places?"

"You'll think I'm crazy if I tell you."

"No, please," Jane insisted.

"My mother had a photograph of her grandparents. They were standing in front of their store. It was here in Cedarville."

"Then let me be the first to welcome you home," said a voice from behind her.

Laurel wheeled around to find herself staring into the dark, brooding eyes of Lucien Caulder.

# CHAPTER 2

The following Saturday morning, after breakfast at Belle Rouge, Laurel drove Eva and Jane to the Salt River Sale Barn, where an unusually large crowd had gathered for the annual county homecoming.

"Sorry, ma'am, this lot is full," said the security guard. "You'll have to park down the street and walk back."

"Why don't you two get out," Laurel suggested. "I have an errand to run in town and I'll meet you back here in about a half hour."

The honking horn behind them helped Eva and Jane make the hasty decision to get out of the car and Laurel quickly drove off.

"We should have stayed together," Jane said as they walked into the grounds.

"Oh, she'll be all right," Eva answered. "Anyway, I think she was looking for an excuse not to come to the flea market."

Forty five minutes later, with her business in town finished, Laurel parked the car in a vacant spot close to the last row of stalls at the sale barn. She realized that because of the impatient driver behind them, they had not designated an exact meeting place. Surely she would eventually run into them in one of the aisles.

Laurel was beginning to see the futility of trying to find her friends in the endless sea of stalls crammed full of pumpkins, gourds and Indian corn, when she spotted what she considered to be some of the finest pieces she had ever seen in all her years of antique hunting. Not even in North Carolina had she found such well-preserved pre-Civil War furniture. When she inspected the pieces closely, any doubt of authenticity was erased from her mind.

In her excitement she hardly noticed the small elderly black man who was smiling at her and her childlike enthusiasm. "Howdy, ma'am. You like ole Barney's merchandise? Ever since I heard someone bought the Kilgore place I figured they'd be here sooner or later."

"How did you know it was me?"

"Word gets around in a town no bigger than this. It's not easy to keep secrets here."

"You have some excellent pieces, but I notice you don't have a complete set of anything. If only that dining room suite had the two captain's chairs. And why in the world would anyone cut off the top of that high-backed bed?"

"It had the family crest on it, ma'am. Rumor has it one of the Kilgores destroyed everything with the crest on it."

"But why would anyone do that?"

The old man's face grew serious. "Some things are lost with time, ma'am."

"So. You mean to tell me all this furniture came from Belle Rouge? How did you get it?"

"My Grand-daddy. Don't rightly know how he got it. Every year I bring the furniture to the homecoming thinking it might find its proper owner. I keep the price so high that no wrong person could buy it."

"Do you think I'm the right person?"

"Ma'am, if you bought Belle Rouge, you are the rightful owner."

Eva and Jane were standing by the front gate when Laurel found them. "I hope I didn't keep you waiting too long," she apologized.

"No, we've just now finished looking," Eva answered. "But we were beginning to worry about you."

"Oh, I've been looking around, too, and you were right. This is an interesting place. Didn't you find anything you wanted to buy?"

"No, nothing," Jane replied.

"Well, I guess I made up for both of you. My errand in town was to buy a tractor and bush hog. And when I came back to the sale barn and started looking for you, I ran into a most interesting find."

Eva's eyes brightened. "What was it?"

"It's some of the original furniture from Belle Rouge. Come on, I'll show you. The man said he'd deliver it Monday."

Hurriedly, Laurel led them down the aisle, where she stopped at the last booth. "That's funny. He was here just a few minutes ago. I guess there was no need for him to stay, since I bought him out," she laughed.

"Maybe we could come over Monday and see the furniture when it's delivered," Jane said.

"Of course you're welcome. But if my tractor is delivered late this afternoon, like the store said it would be, I might be mowing in back of the barn. Just come on down there and give me a yell."

"You're not going to mow when there's no one there with you, are you?" Eva frowned.

"I'll be fine."

"The field will be too wet with dew until midmorning. Don't start till Jane and I get there."

At ten o'clock Monday morning, Eva knocked on the front door of the mansion at Belle Rouge. When there was no response, she and Jane proceeded to the back door. Again there was no answer.

"Look, there behind the barn," Jane exclaimed.

The almost comical figure proudly bounced along on the new John Deere, dressed in faded jeans, old plaid shirt and sweat-banded hat pulled down so far that it showed only a rim of her reddish blonde hair. Laurel waved and headed the tractor toward the house.

"I thought I told you to wait for us," Eva scolded.

"There wasn't any dew this morning. Besides, I have to learn to do things for myself."

"You're one stubborn woman, Laurel Mackenzie."

"I've been told that many times before. Come in and look at the new furniture," she said, turning off the engine. "Barney delivered it early this morning. I had him put it on the second floor."

"How could an elderly man carry furniture up these stairs?" Jane asked.

"Barney's very strong, and I helped him."

"You're going to overdo it and make yourself sick."

"Eva, you sound just like my mother used to." Laurel led them to a large room on the second story. "Here's the furniture. What do you think?"

"Oh, it's beautiful," Jane exclaimed. "It must have cost you a fortune."

"No, on the contrary, Barney gave it to me for next to nothing."

Curiosity led Eva toward the staircase leading to the glass-enclosed room on top of the mansion. "Have you been up there yet?" she asked.

"No," Laurel answered, "and I have no desire to."

"Would you mind if I painted up there sometime?" Eva asked. "I love to paint watercolors and I bet there's a wonderful view from up there."

Laurel felt the queasiness return. "No, I wouldn't mind."

Eva inched her way up the stairs to where she could reach the door. "It's been nailed shut."

"Leave it alone," Laurel snapped. "It must be dangerous up there or it wouldn't be nailed."

"Let's just see," Eva persisted. "The view has to be breathtaking from that height. Think about it. If we go up there, you can see the results of all your mowing. I saw a crowbar over in the corner of the room. Get it for me, Jane."

"That's strange," Jane said. "The room on this side of the staircase is smaller than the one on the other side."

"You're right," Eva agreed, taking the crowbar from her. "There should be a window in the small room. I know I can see a window from the outside."

"If that's so, someone has walled up this end of the room," Laurel replied. "It must be like the glass room, closed for a reason. Please, Eva, come down."

"Now, who's being the worried mother? I've almost got it open. I can't stop when I'm this close."

Judging by the age of the nails and the handmade brackets, Eva was certain the door had been sealed for many years. The minute it opened she knew she was being covered by dust from a different era. Hastily, Eva climbed up into the glass enclosed room. "You should see the view from here!" she cried. "Come on, you two. It's wonderful."

"Go on," Jane urged Laurel. "I'm right behind you."

Laurel couldn't quite determine if it was because of the heat and humidity, or because she had been working so hard, but suddenly she felt faint.

"Are you all right?" Jane asked.

Laurel wiped the sweat from her face, sat down and leaned back against the glass wall. "Yes, just let me rest a minute."

"Look, it's starting to rain," Eva said. "Isn't it beautiful? Belle Rouge looks like some French impressionist painting through the rain and these old window panes."

"It's magnificent," Jane sighed. "Laurel, don't you think it's just the most..."

She turned to see Laurel clutching the railing, her face pale and sweaty, her eyes glazed. "Dear God! Sit back down and put your head between your knees."

"I have to get out of here! Help me down the ladder."

"You're in no condition to get on a ladder. Let me get you a glass of tea," Eva said.

"And I'll get a cold cloth," Jane offered.

Before Laurel could respond, both women were down the stairs and out of sight. Then, she heard an unfamiliar voice.

"Boy, get back on that horse!"

"Jane! Eva! Someone's out back. I hear them talking."

When no response came, Laurel pulled herself to her knees and wiped a pane of glass to peer toward the back of the house. She thought she could make out an oval ring in the field by the barn which had not been discernible at ground level.

The voice came again. "There's not another horse in Kentucky that can beat this crimson devil!"

"It's a race track!" Laurel exclaimed. When she wiped the pane again, she could make out the words painted on the barn...*Belle Rouge: Home of Red Satan*. Then she saw them. A black jockey was being given a leg up on a prancing red stallion by a tall, dark man.

The red stallion's long legs carried him effortlessly around the track and into the homestretch. "Barnabas! Don't let him bear out! Keep him in tight."

The jockey pulled out a whip concealed under his left arm, raised it high in the air and hit the stallion a sharp blow on its right shoulder. The horse veered away from the whip, while the jockey grabbed for its mane, desperately trying to keep his seat. But the full weight of the horse's body fell against the rail, and the fence gave way. The animal hit the ground with a thud and rolled over, barely missing the prostrate rider.

The tall man's stride quickly took him to where the stallion was struggling to get up. He grabbed the reins, pulled the horse to its feet and tied it to the post. His jaw was set in anger as he picked up the whip and stood towering above the dazed jockey. "I'll show you what to do with a whip, you idiot!" The whip came down on the young black man's back with such force he fell to his knees. "I've told you never to hit a horse of mine." Again the whip found its target.

"I'm sorry, Mr. Kilgore, I'm sorry," the jockey apologized.

A petite girl with long golden hair ran across the track and threw her arms around the man's waist, placing herself between him and the black man. "Don't hit Barnabas again. Please, Daddy."

"Claire, keep out of this!"

"Please, leave him alone. We must see to Red Satan."

Kilgore's anger subsided at the thought of his prized stallion. But with one final statement, he pointed the whip at the black man. "Don't you ever go against my orders again or you'll live to regret it."

Claire Kilgore stroked the stallion's neck while her father ran his hand gently over the horse's knees and ankles. "Lead him around, daughter. Let's see if he favors that left leg."

"He seems to be fine, Daddy. He's so strong, it would take more than a fall to hurt him."

"We're lucky nothing bad happened. I didn't keep his sire and dam hidden from the rebels for four years just to lose him when some boy disobeys my orders. This horse is the best chance we've ever had to win the Gold Cup." A slight smile played at the corner of Kilgore's lips. "You will have to say that Red Satan is starting to live up to his name."

"Daddy, could you please come to the house and talk to Momma. She's been watching from the observatory, and you know she's bound to have one of her spells after all this excitement."

Kilgore looked up toward the glass enclosure on top of the house. Even from that distance, Laurel could feel his riveting stare. She felt like a bird trapped in a cage.

As the man disappeared around the corner of the house, her attention was drawn back to the barn, where Barnabas untied the horse's reins with a snap. Wild eyed at the sound, the animal arched his neck, reared and struck at the black man with his front hooves. Barnabas yanked the horse's head down. "Whoa, you red devil!"

A statuesque mulatto woman leaned against the stall door, watching the dancing stallion follow the limping jockcy to the stable. "Better not let Mr. Sumner see you jerk Satan in the mouth."

Barnabas undid the girth and placed the saddle across the railing. "I gotta teach this horse some manners or he gonna hurt somebody bad."

"You mark what I tell you, little man. Mr. Sumner Kilgore loves his horses better than anything, or anybody. So you best be careful how you treat 'em."

The black man picked up a cloth and began to rub the stallion's glistening coat. "I'd say he loves Miss Claire, Miz Kilgore and Mr. Ross, first."

The woman's eyes narrowed. "If you think that, you are dead wrong. I know him better than anybody." She walked a few steps away from the barn where she could see Sumner Kilgore and his daughter entering the house. "Look at her up there," she pointed toward the glass enclosed room. "She's crazy. Miz Kilgore's out of her mind. Do you think Mr. Sumner could love anybody like her? He needs a strong woman."

"Like you?" Barnabas asked, lifting the stallion's hoof and picking it clean.

Ignoring the remark, the woman continued. "And Mr. Ross? All he wants to do is paint pictures, just like his mother. Mr. Sumner deserves a son who'll run this farm. It's a disgrace that Miz Kilgore bore him a child like Mr. Ross."

"Genevieve! Shut your mouth! I'm not gonna let any wife of mine talk about Miss Lily and Mr. Ross that way."

"Wife of yours? I will never be a wife to you. You never have touched me, and you never will."

"I'm aware of the 'arrangement', woman. But you got no right..."

"I got every right," Genevieve seethed.

Barnabas undid the stallion and placed him in the stall. Calmly, he turned to face her. "If you think you got any rights with Mr. Kilgore, you're mistaken. The only place you got with him is in his bed and that's whenever HE says so. Don't you get no ideas---like YOU could be mistress of Belle Rouge. Miss

Claire's the one who'll get this farm when something happens to Mr. Kilgore. He'll leave it to her."

"Humph! She won't stay here. Mr. Sumner tries to hold her too tight. She'll marry the first man who comes along, just to get away from him."

"You sound like you got this all figured out, but you ain't, Gen. I give you the same warnin' you give me. Don't ever cross Mr. Kilgore. You're no more to him than a whore and a whore can be replaced without no trouble at all."

"Don't you never call me that! I know who he loves and I know who deserves to be by his side....it's me. And nobody's gonna keep me from it...not you, not Miss Lily, Mr. Ross, or Miss Claire. Nobody gonna stop me!

"Don't you never try to pull none of your fool 'stuff' on this family!"

"I don't know what you're talking about."

"I seen you. You foolin' with evil and it's gonna backfire on you. Leave it alone, I tell you." Barnabas took the saddle and bridle, placed them in the tack room, then headed for the house. "Come on. It's time we got dinner on the table."

Genevieve smiled as she reached into her pocket and slipped the red stallion some sugar. "He trying to tell me what to do, but he's too late, ain't he, red devil? Me and you already got an agreement. Ain't nobody gonna stand in our way."

It was Eva's voice that drew Laurel back. "Are you all right? You must have fainted."

"Did you hear someone out back?" Laurel asked. "I tried to get up. I heard voices and I saw..."

"Oh, dear! You're burning up with fever," Jane exclaimed. "Let's get you into bed."

The storm clouds had passed, and the sun was radiating through the window when Laurel awoke sometime later.

"Are you feeling better?" Eva asked.

"Much better. How long have I been asleep?"

"Several hours."

"I guess I'm just exhausted." After a brief pause, Laurel continued. "But the strangest thing happened while I was alone in the observatory."

"It couldn't have been as strange as the talking you've been doing in your sleep," Eva added.

"What did I say?"

"Something about a race track out by the barn and a red stallion."

Laurel bolted upright in bed. "That's what I saw from the observatory."

"When your fever broke and you seemed to be sleeping peacefully, I decided to investigate what you were mumbling about," Jane said. "The rain made it easy to see the outline of a race track in the back field. And I could barely make it out, but on the side of the barn I saw the name---*Red Satan.*"

## CHAPTER 3

On the afternoon of the day Laurel ran an ad in the local newspaper, a knock came at the back door. A smile crossed her face when she saw the small, black gentleman standing on the stoop. “Barney!” she grabbed his hand. “I’m so happy to see you again.”

“I came about your ad for a handyman, Miz Mackenzie.”

“Come in, and I’ll tell you what I want done.”

She caught his hesitation. “It’s all right, come in and sit down.” She poured two large glasses of iced tea. “Sweetened or unsweetened?” she asked.

“Whatever’s convenient, ma’am.”

Laurel sat down across from her guest and pushed the sugar bowl toward him. “Before we do anything else,” she said, “we need to get some things straight. If I ask you if you want sugar or not, you tell me what you want. If I ask you what you think, tell me what you think. When we start our project, if I tell you something I want done and it’s wrong to do it my way---tell me.”

Barney’s eyes twinkled and he shook his head in glee. “You kinda tell it like it is, don’t you, Miz Mackenzie? I sure ’nuff like that. Now, to answer your question. Yes, ma’am, I do want sugar. In fact, I want TWO spoons full.”

“Good, good,” Laurel laughed out loud. “We’re going to make a great team. I can’t wait to tell you about our project.”

The jangling of the phone abruptly put an end to the conversation. It was the call Laurel had hoped for since beginning her writing career.

"Hello, Laurel," came the voice of her agent. "I've got some good news. A Hollywood studio wants to buy the rights to your last novel! They've agreed for you to collaborate on the screen-play."

"I can't believe it," she replied. "I thought after the first two books hit the bestseller list and weren't picked up, this third one didn't have a prayer."

"Well, that's Hollywood---no one can second guess them. However, this is not an offer for a movie---not just yet. They love your story line, but they aren't happy with your dialogue. Come to California and work with one of their writers."

"How long do I have before I have to give you an answer?"

"What do you mean, how long? They want to know when you can start, not if you accept. Come on, Laurel, you can't afford not to---if you want to further your career."

"I don't mean to stall, but I've just started what will become my best work, ever. This new book is flowing. I'm not having to think up the story line, I can't type as fast as the words are coming. It's as if this story must be told."

"All right. I realize you're coming out of the slump, but if you take this offer, you'll have your foot in the door, and that new work will stand an even better chance of making it big."

"When would I start, and how much time are we talking about?"

"They want to start in two weeks and they'll give you three to work on it. If you're back to your old self again, it'll be done on time. Hollywood and the world are just waiting for *Beyond Revelation."*

Laurel rejoined Barney at the table. "I hope fixing that chimney out back into a barbecue will take us only about two weeks. That's all I've got before I have to leave town."

"We can get it done in one week, ma'am."

Laurel and Barney attacked their work with a relentless drive. "Ma'am, you won't have to buy no flagstone. There's rock on the back of this place that'll be just perfect. Now, wait a minute Miz Mackenzie, we're gonna have to dig down and make a footer for this wall. It ain't gonna last when there's freezing weather if we don't. You don't have to buy no concrete mix, I got some on my truck. You don't need to buy no flowers to plant, there's plenty of wild ones back by the creek."

The joy of their accomplishments kept Laurel's mind from hearing the accumulation of all Barney had said in the past week. But on the final day of their work, when he was cleaning up and Laurel had gone into the house to fix them some lunch, his last and most important statement came.

"Miz Mackenzie, look here what I found!"

"Where did you get that?" she asked.

Barney led her to the side of the fireplace, where he pulled out one of the stones. "Look, ma'am, it's a secret place, and this little book was in it. It sure must be old from the looks of it."

Laurel took the book from him. "Oh my! It appears to be a diary."

As she started to open it, Barney said, "I gotta go now, I gotta be somewhere else."

"Yes, of course," she answered, her concentration centered on the prize in her hands.

She looked up in time to see the dust boiling up from behind Barney's old dilapidated truck. "Wait, wait! I haven't paid you! Oh well, I guess you'll be back when you need the money."

With the book in her hand, she sat down in one of the wrought iron chairs on the new patio that surrounded the old fireplace. Carefully, she opened it. *Diary of Lily Rossini*, the words were delicately penned. Laurel began reading the first entry.

*February 20, 1857*

*My life is about to tread upon a new avenue. Due to the tragic loss of my parents a year ago, I will soon take the last name of a man I hardly know. So I will never forget who I was, I start this journey as Lily Rossini. The distinctive coloratura soprano voice of my mother and the echoes of the Steinway so gently played by my dear father filled our gracious home in New Orleans. It was a place of gaiety and love. My finest painting to date is a picture of Mother, with a single tear upon her cheek, seated on the lower steps of the entrance to the house, wearing a costume from a Rossini opera. The director of La Scala pleaded that such beauty and pathos must be given a prominent place in his theatre. Thus, hanging just to the left of the center aisle doors is my painting of my exquisite mother.*

*My revered father's resemblance I could never capture on canvas, for I regarded father from within. I*

*worshipped him and must preserve these emotions for no other...not even the man I am to marry, the tenacious horseman from Kentucky---Sumner Kilgore.*

"Oh, dear god," Laurel caught her breath. "Sumner. I know that's the name of the man I saw when I was in the glass room. Jane and Eva never told me Kilgore's first name. I didn't know what it was." Eagerly, she read on.

*March 16, 1857*

*I could not wed and leave New Orleans without presenting a proper society wedding. Thus, Sumner*

*spared no expense in hiring the best caterers, musicians and decorators. There were white ribbons on each of the iron posts that lined the carriage circle. Hundreds of lilies were brought in from the Orient and placed around the gazebo, where the wedding was to take place. In the bright May sunshine, the house seemed to glow with whiteness. Looking down from the second story balcony, the gardens gave one a mystical sensation, a dreamlike state of mind. This same abstractedness had engulfed me for the past two months.*

*I met Sumner Kilgore at the funeral of a dear friend's father. For more than four decades, the Kilgore family's trading company had maintained direct shipping to and from the coast of China. The company brought in tons of rice, silks and spices in trade for tobacco, sugar cane and hemp. It was the hemp that brought Mr. Kilgore to New Orleans twice a year. Apparently, there could not be any finer rope hemp than that grown in Kentucky and supplied by the Kilgore farm. In fact, the trading company would not accept hemp from any other grower.*

*Sumner's father established the relationship with the company and Sumner has continued it, more than doubling the wealth his father left him. After the funeral, I allowed Sumner to escort me to my friend's home to pay my respects. It was on this short journey I realized that somehow I must capture the heart of Sumner Kilgore. I had attended enough operas to know how to intrigue a young protagonist. I had not the need to perform such an aria while my parents were alive, but without Mother and Father I have neither the support nor the strength to survive on my own. Mr. Kilgore extended his stay in New Orleans for two weeks, and I accompanied him to dinner, the opera, the theatre, and boat excursions on the Mississippi River. I became the woman adaptable to any setting. Sumner was intrigued by my stories of Europe and my knowledge of art. I, in return, showed the greatest of interest in his favorite sport, horseracing. I thank God he never asked me to go riding with him. I have such a terror of horses that I never so much as sat on one.*

*Yesterday, the day Sumner was to leave for Kentucky, he stated his love for me and wished the honor of my hand in marriage. I was so elated that I kissed him for the first time. It was at this moment I knew the elation was out of gratitude, not love.*

*I suppose this is why I see this mystic aura looking down at my wedding garden. Mr. Kilgore has acquired my respect and admiration, but not my love. I pray to God that I may become the wife he deserves.*

*April 10, 1859*

*Oh, but springtime does instill within me a rebirth of creativity. It is said that the great painters of Europe would choose a subject and then create on canvas what their hearts felt. I understand this philosophy while looking at Belle Rouge. Sumner has constructed what my mind and heart drew on paper. Turning into the lane at the two large stone entrance pillars, the first stimulation comes from the sight of the dogwood and redbud trees that grow wild in abundance on the farm. I had never experienced these before.*

*As one reaches the top of a small knoll, the house, my house, comes into view. It is at this point my breath escapes me and the beauty in my sight overwhelms me. Through the newly crimson maple trees lies our Italian-influenced home. The maples end at a large circular carriage drive, with the center containing the most beautiful display of Kentucky wildflowers that Barnabas could find. What would we ever do without the gardening hand of Barnabas?*

*The house is positioned on the highest ground of the entire 1,500 acres to overlook the gentle roll of the land and a range of hills, called knobs, on the south. The house is two stories tall, with the third floor being small and enclosed in glass. The front of the house features a double door entrance and a cathedral-style window that reaches from floor to ceiling and spans approximately sixteen feet in width, a statement unseen in Kentucky, I dare say. How serene it looks, our Belle Rouge. On the west side of the entrance lies the music room and on the east side, the formal sitting room. There is a library, a gracious dining room and three bedrooms on this floor as well. The kitchen is through the dogtrot at the rear of the house. The second floor is very unusual, for there are only four rooms, three being bedrooms and the final, smaller room, my studio. The walls on the latter are double in thickness to muffle any distractions. In keeping with the times, we also included the glass room forming the third floor, more for my enjoyment than as a slave observatory.*

*The brick is a deep coral, a burnt red that is made in this area of the state. This was one point Sumner was not to be moved on. He felt the house was foreign looking enough and using locally made brick somehow made it feel, what he called "less ostentatious." Ostentatious or not, the house is constructed to last for many generations of Kilgores.*

When the sun began to disappear behind the hills and Laurel could no longer see the words written on the page, she closed the book. "Lily Kilgore," she said the name out loud. "I can't believe it. I have a diary written by a woman who was the wife of the original owner of Belle Rouge."

Stiftly, she got up from the chair on the patio and hurried toward the house, eager to find its warmth on this cool October night. Quickly, she showered, put on her gown, propped herself up with pillows and once again opened the diary.

*January 6, 1860*

*My child, when you are born there will be so much I will want to tell you about your heritage and what influence it will have upon your life. I pray you will enjoy the finer things life has to offer: the theatre, the opera, and most especially, the world of visual art. Since I have been in Kentucky, I have not felt the calling to the canvas. I suppose it may be due to the work we have done on the house. But creative in my mind I have not been, and without the mind's eye I could not possibly paint.*

*Contentment. I do not know if I have obtained this phase in life. Happiness. I long ago gave up hope. But I so much want to display love to my family---my life's work. Dr. James told me I would have periods of depression and that I should concentrate on your birth and everything would be fine. Thus far, the plan has not worked. The only female Sumner has attended to during gestation is one of his broodmares. His attention to me is not even the same he shows to one of these mares, except my doctor is not a veterinarian. I have tried to tell your father what it is that I need...his love and understanding. I know he has trouble with emotional display. If only he had had the opportunity to study my father.*

*Even into their forties, my parents acted as young lovers. When I think of them, I see Father seated at the piano, and mother standing behind him with her hands placed lovingly upon his shoulders while singing one of her beautiful melodies. At the end of the singing, she would sit beside him, and they would embrace an embrace of love. I so envy their affection for each other.*

*If you are a boy--and I know you are, your name will be---*

Before she could turn the page, Laurel said the name aloud. "Ross---his name is Ross."

The sun was coming up before Laurel put the diary down again. After a few hours of sleep, she awoke and without taking time to dress, she went to her desk and began to write.

Chapter after chapter of her new book was completed over the next days, but at a high personal price to Laurel. Her work became an obsession. There was little time to eat or sleep, and though she was thankful the phone hardly rang, allowing her the privacy to write, she was a bit concerned about what appeared to be a growing 'heaviness' around her. Perhaps it was simply the loneliness often experienced by every writer. But even as she tried to convince herself of this, she knew it was more than that. She actually heard the 'sounds' the real estate agent had mentioned. But most importantly, day by day she felt 'them', her characters, moving more freely in the old house.

It was an exhausted Laurel Mackenzie who met Jane at the door on the morning Jane was to drive her to the airport. "Laurel, what's wrong with you?" she asked.

"I'm just tired. I've been writing quite a bit," was all the answer Laurel could manage.

Jane respected her need for quietness and it was not until they pulled to a stop in front of the terminal that Laurel spoke again. "Jane, may I ask a favor of you? Do you think you might edit my manuscript for grammar and punctuation, while I'm gone? Of course, I'll pay you."

"I'm flattered you asked. I'd love to do it."

"Here's a key to the house. Everything's on my desk."

After leaving Laurel at the airport, Jane made a stop at Eva's house. "Laurel looks awful," she told her. "She's been pushing herself re-doing Belle Rouge and now she's been staying up all hours working on her new book."

"We're going to have to keep a closer eye on her when she returns from California," Eva added.

"She wants me to edit her new book. Of course, I said yes immediately. But now I'm not sure. I'm not qualified to do that."

"I don't know who'd be better at it. You did teach English for thirty years."

"But this is a novel."

"Is it written in English?" Eva teased.

"Of course it is."

"Then you ought to know correct punctuation and grammar. It'll be a cinch for you."

"Maybe you're right. Just think. I'll know what happens in a Laurel Mackenzie mystery before anyone else does!"

"You'd better let your best friend know, too," Eva laughed.

At mid-afternoon the next day, Eva's phone rang. "Can you come over to Belle Rouge?" Jane's voice asked.

"Of course, what's wrong?"

"Just come over, and hurry."

"What's all this about?" Eva asked as she followed Jane into Laurel's study.

Jane handed her a chapter. "Read this. Take a look at the names."

Eva read for a few seconds, then lay the chapter down. "My god, how could she know?"

Three weeks later, the screenplay finished, Laurel boarded the plane for home. She only nodded in response to the stewardess's greeting. "Thank goodness the plane's not as crowded as the flight out was," she thought to herself. She spotted several rows of seats over the wing where no one had chosen to sit. Quickly she moved to the window seat and placed her jacket in the middle seat of the three to discourage anyone from sitting close to her.

Though she had long since realized she must use the airlines to expedite her travels, she still could not consent to liking it. She felt her stomach tighten as the plane started to pull away from the gate. She closed her eyes, gripped the arms of her seat and took a deep breath.

"May I sit with you?" she heard a soft voice.

"Of course," Laurel replied.

A regal woman with copper colored skin and jet black hair, pulled back into a bun, slid into the aisle seat. "There's no need to move your jacket, I'll be quite comfortable here."

Self-consciously, she returned the woman's smile, for Laurel realized she had been staring at her. She wasn't a particularly beautiful woman. Her face was long and her features angular, but there was something compelling about her.

"You don't care for flying," the woman stated, rather than asked.

"No, but I'll be all right as soon as we're airborne," Laurel replied.

"We already are," the woman smiled curiously.

Laurel looked out of the window and realized the plane had leveled off. "Well, how about that," she sighed.

A twinkle came to the woman's eye. "Strange, what the mind can do, isn't it? What we don't know, can't hurt us. What we do know---might."

"I beg your pardon?"

"Just a little Cajun philosophy, Laurel Mackenzie."

"How did you know my...?"

"I saw your briefcase under the seat in front of you. Your name's engraved on it."

For some unexplained reason, Laurel picked up the briefcase and held it tightly.

"You are a writer, are you not?" the woman questioned.

"How did you…?"

This time the woman laughed. "I've read all your books."

Soon Laurel found herself feeling quite comfortable with her fellow passenger. "You mentioned Cajun a moment ago," she said. "Is that the slight accent I detect?"

"Yes, I'm originally from New Orleans."

"What a coincidence. My new book starts out in New Orleans."

"You live in Kentucky. Why write of New Orleans? I hear your state has a lot of folklore."

"How did you know I moved to...?"

"Miss Mackenzie, our plane makes one stop before continuing to New York City, and it's in Louisville. I don't see you having business in, or living in, New York."

Laurel leaned back when she realized she was sitting on the edge of her seat. She had to take a moment to sift through this woman's words. In a short time she was ready to ask some questions.

"You know my name. May I ask yours?"

"Nila. Simply Nila."

"Are you going to New York?"

"I go, Miss Mackenzie, where I'm led."

Laurel raised her eyebrow. "Why were you led to this particular...?"

"To meet someone."

"Miss...ah...Nila, you seem to know what I'm going to ask before I ask it. Have we met before?"

"Before what, Miss Mackenzie?"

"You talk in riddles."

"Yes, and I have one for you.

*Of all the things we can define,*
*Who will dare to explain - TIME?*
*Is it past? Is it now? Is it future, and if so, how?*
*Dare to not answer with the mind.*
*Dare to seek and you will find.*
*Do words once said, still live,*
*Or are they buried among the dead?*
*Can the eye ever recall Images faint, against a wall?*
*The spirit can travel, and it can roam,*
*But answers are found, close to home."*

"I don't have the foggiest notion what you're talking about."

"I know you don't, Miss Mackenzie, but it will be made clear to you."

"I'll never be able to remember the words of your poem, so how can I solve the riddle?"

Nila shoved a folded piece of paper toward Laurel's hand. "Here, I wrote it down for you. Now, if you will excuse me, I need to go to the lavatory." The woman gracefully rose from her seat. "Till we meet again," she smiled.

Eva and Jane were waiting for Laurel when she disembarked from the plane. "Did you have a good trip?" Eva asked.

"Yes, and I met the most interesting woman on the way back."

"Oh, we've had an interesting time, too. Eva helped me on the editing of your book."

"That's great. How do you like it? I think the plot is one of my best."

"There's something more interesting in it than the plot," Jane said.

"What?" Laurel asked.

"Eva and I want to know how you got the names Preston Miller and Timothy James for two of your characters. Those are the names of our great-grandfathers."

# CHAPTER 4

The day after her flight back from California, Laurel drove to Eva's house to share Lily Kilgore's diary with her. She found Eva's quaint, story-and-a-half cottage nestled underneath aging oak trees on the last street within the Cedarville city limits. Jane's car was already in the driveway.

Eva led her down the hallway and past the living room, where some previous day's newspaper was still scattered across the floor. The large framed picture over the couch hung slightly askew and the older television sat forlornly in the corner, its rabbit-eared antenna pointing to nine o'clock.

The dining room table was home to numerous stacks of papers, and the antique sideboard on the far wall collected various and sundry knick-knacks, candle holders, and small pieces of silver. Among the clutter in the china cabinet, Laurel spotted some exquisite pieces of crystal. In the kitchen, the breakfast dishes had been washed and placed haphazardly in the drainer to dry, and a bulging black plastic trash bag sat by the back door.

Eva pushed aside the opened envelopes, the sugar bowl and the salt and pepper shakers on the kitchen table to make a place for the diary, while the frown on Jane's face grew more and more intense. "If it would make you happier," Eva said to her, "you can collect all this junk and put it on the counter."

"It would give us more room," Jane replied.

Eva turned to Laurel. "You should see her house. Everything's in place and not a speck of dust anywhere. My house drives her crazy."

"You could have a cleaning lady come in once a week, as I do," Jane shot back.

"I have everything out where I can find it. I don't want anybody fooling around in my things. Besides, we Pisces are supposed to have homes that look like kaleidoscopes."

"Your house certainly fits that description."

"Jane really likes my house. She's here most every day."

Laurel was amazed at the camaraderie between these two women. They were total opposites, and though their teasing was with barbed tongue, they were comfortable and compatible with each other. She wondered why they seemed so eager to include her.

"We want you around because we like you," Eva said.

The startled look on Laurel's face caused Eva to continue. "You were wondering why we invited you into our friendship, weren't you?"

"That's exactly what I was thinking. How did you...? Oh, I forgot, you're psychic."

"You don't believe in psychic ability?" Jane asked.

"I don't know anything about it."

"Well, that's a discussion for another day," Eva said. "You did bring the diary?"

Laurel took the book from her purse and placed it on the table. "I want to read out loud an entry Lily made that concerns both your great-grandfathers."

*December 20, 1865*

*As I look back over the last years, I am thankful we have survived this great civil war intact, though the conflict came very near to us. General Morgan and his band of guerrillas came as close as the railroad junction and there was a skirmish at the railway bridge in Cedarville. Only once did the confederates set foot on Belle Rouge. Sheriff Preston Miller was in the Confederate Army during the first years of the war and it was due to his persuasion that our farm was not robbed of its stock.*

*Sumner, though his sympathies were with the North, did not serve in the army. He paid someone to take his place. He felt the protection of Belle Rouge was more important than the survival of the Union.*

*It was not my husband who watched over me during these trying times. It was Doctor James. He has seen me through three miscarriages, and he has tended my son, Ross, with the same dedication. If only Sumner were like him.*

*I am not sure Timothy's wife appreciates him any more than my husband does me. He has confided in me that he did not marry her for love, but because of the urging of his family. He does, however, have three handsome sons. I am particularly taken with the youngest. He is very much like his father. I have not been able to give my husband the kind of son he so desperately wants. He despises the fact that Ross belongs entirely to me. He shows nothing of his father's love of horses, but he shows every indication that he is very talented in painting. Even at this young age, he sits, hour upon hour, with brush and canvas. Sumner cannot hide the disgust in his eyes for both me and my son. I am now in the seventh month of pregnancy. How desperately I want this baby, but I have great fear for it. There is no way this child will please Sumner. I can only surrender the consequences to God.*

As Laurel closed the diary, Eva spoke. "What is Lily talking about, 'surrender the consequences to God?'"

"I don't know, but can't you feel the fear in her words?" Laurel shuddered.

"Did Lily have the second child?" Jane asked.

"Yes. It was a girl."

"Her name was Claire. Wasn't it?"

Yes, Eva. The same name I heard from the glass room."

"It's remarkable. Every name you mentioned the day you got sick in the glass room is the name of someone in the Kilgore family."

Laurel felt the chill again. "This whole thing frightens me. I don't know what's happening. These people are becoming so real. I can usually identify with the characters I use in my books, but these people are more than that. When I first started to write, my agent warned me not to get too wrapped up in my characters' lives. He said it could be dangerous. I was able to do that until now, but I can't seem to shake these people off, even when I'm not at my typewriter."

"I know nothing about characters or writing," Eva said. "But I do know of several people who have moved into a house where a lot of strife had gone on and they experienced visitations from previous occupants."

"You mean ghosts?" Laurel asked. "I don't see ghosts. I'm just identifying with these people---especially Lily."

"We could have an exorcism of the house," Eva offered. "There's a professor at the university who's an acquaintance of mine. He's done extensive research and he has friends who do that sort..."

"No!" Laurel interrupted. "I want no such thing. I could never do that."

"Are you afraid of losing your characters?" Jane asked.

"Maybe. But, it's more than that. I can't explain it."

"Just promise you'll be careful."

"How can I do that, Eva, when I don't even know what I'm supposed to fear?"

"Just please know that you can talk to either of us, at any time," Eva said. "Don't ever think we would tell anyone what you say, and know that nothing you could say would influence our friendship in any way."

"Thank you. I really appreciate both of you."

"Now, is there anything else in Lily's diary that you feel we may need to know?" Jane asked.

"There are just sporadic entries over the next years. But Lily often mentions a wealthy woman named Alexandra Lennox from Louisville."

"The owner of the Lennox Hotel and theatre?" Jane asked.

"Yes. Do you know of her?"

"I don't have many things of Preston Miller's, because the 1937 flood destroyed most of what we had of his, but there are a few of his documents and letters remaining. If I remember correctly, one was from Mrs. Lennox."

"Do you remember what was in it?" Laurel questioned.

"Yes, I do. Mrs. Lennox wrote of her concern for a young lady named Claire. Was it Claire Kilgore?"

"For Claire, and not Lily?" Laurel asked.

Jane nodded. Then Laurel continued. "Lily wrote that Mrs. Lennox periodically brought her to Louisville to enjoy the arts she loved so well. In fact, the last entry in the diary speaks of Alexandra." Laurel thumbed through the book. "This entry is dated *February 10, 1882*. Ross was twenty-two and Claire would have been fifteen. I'll read what Lily wrote."

*How fortunate my children and I are to count Alexandra as a friend. Ross returned today from visiting her and she has arranged with the museum in Louisville to exhibit his paintings.*

*Both Alexandra and Ross have encouraged me to include some of mine, but I cannot. Sumner would be furious. I must do everything I can to keep peace in this family no matter what the cost.*

"Is there anything else of importance in the diary?" Eva asked.

"Lily despised Genevieve, the mulatto woman who was Barnabas' wife. She mentions that Genevieve carried a baby boy full term, but he died a few days later. She talks of her own failing health and of Doctor James attending her. She speaks of Sumner's drinking."

"From what I know of my great-grandfather, he drank with Sumner Kilgore," Jane sighed.

"Yes. Lily said as much, but she respected Preston Miller."

"What's the date of the last entry in the diary?" Eva asked.

*"February 10, 1882.*

"That's strange," Eva said. "That date sticks in my mind. My great-grandfather records that Lily and Ross both died on February 12, 1882. That would be two days after Ross visited Mrs. Lennox." Eva said.

"Does Doctor James say what happened?" Laurel questioned.

"Not in detail."

Absentmindedly, Laurel thumbed through Lily's diary until Jane stopped her. "Wait," she exclaimed. "Look on the back pages. There's more writing."

"I didn't see that," Laurel said. "I assumed the diary stopped at these blank pages."

"Read what it says," Eva suggested.

*Devil Red has done the deed. The end will come for this seed. White dove tries her best to fly. With no wings, she did die.*

Laurel pushed the diary toward Eva. “The last entry’s not in Lily’s handwriting.”

“You’re right. It’s someone else’s. But whose? Maybe Claire wrote it. Doctor James mentioned that she was a writer.”

“May I read Doctor James’ book now?” Laurel asked.

The phone rang. Eva handed the receiver to Laurel. “It’s for you.”

After a few hurried replies, Laurel hung up. “I had my calls forwarded to your house. That was my agent. He needs some information that’s at my house. I’ll give you a call when I’m finished.”

Eva closed the door behind Laurel and returned to the kitchen.

“What’s wrong with you?” Jane asked.

“Come into the parlor. I want to show you something.”

Eva opened the door to a room that did not seem to be a part of the rest of her house. The soft gray walls provided a background for a Victorian atmosphere. A silky fabric of bold pink roses covered the love seat and chair, and a slight odor of roses came from potpourri burning in a white ceramic pot on the coffee table. Curtains of white French lace moved at the whim of the unusually warm November breeze. The parlor was elegant and orderly.

Eva went to the bookcase and pulled a tattered green book from the shelf. “I have heard through my family, that Dr. James and I share some of the same psychic abilities. Look on the back page. Look at what my great-grandfather wrote,” she said.

Jane read the words aloud:

*In the time of the waning moon*
*When the owl surveys his kingdom of darkness,*
*There shall come to pass*
*The breath of a new wind.*
*But yet it is an old wind*
*That contains within it*
*The knowledge of the ages.*

"What is this?" Jane asked.

"I call it, my great-grandfather's prophecy." Eva's voice was almost inaudible. "I think its time has come."

# CHAPTER 5

Laurel replaced the receiver of the phone in her study, sat back in her chair and sighed. She could hardly believe how her life was beginning to come together. A few years ago, when she wondered if her career would go anywhere, she had shared with her husband her dreams of this very day. Now five years later, three novels were published and a screenplay given the OK, but she would have to experience the joy alone.

She changed into jeans and boots and jumped into the used tan Ranger she had bought when she came back from California. Every farm owner needs a truck, she convinced herself. She smiled when she thought of what her ex-husband would say if he knew she had spent so much money. Laurel headed down the driveway, rolled down the truck window and inhaled the aroma of autumn. This time of year had always stirred something inside her she could not explain. Sometimes it came as a fragmented memory. Sometimes it was the remembrance of a vague dream. Nonetheless, the feeling it caused lingered as a nagging sadness throughout the season.

"But why autumn?" she had often asked herself. It was a time when things were dying, she reasoned. Maybe that was the cause of her sadness. No. When she thought of autumn, she thought of a time when a fireplace welcomed her in from the cold.

Yes, autumn was the season when everyone should enjoy being home.

She released her breath, aware of a lightness in her spirit. For the first time in her life, she was really happy. She did, indeed, feel at home.

Laurel had passed by the faded roadside sign many times on her way in and out of Cedarville. Today, she was purposely going to check out Hickory Ridge Thoroughbred Training Center.

She turned off the main road onto a gravel drive that wound its way to a large red and white barn. In front of the barn lay a half-mile training track, a four-stall starting gate resting in the chute. Several horse trailers were neatly backed against the fence surrounding a paddock.

She parked the Ranger beside a red and gray double cab truck. She saw no one moving about, but in the quiet she could hear the rhythmic galloping of a horse. A horse and rider rounded the turn and headed down the back stretch.

She walked to the opposite side of the barn. A man stood by the rail watching the horse as it passed. Next to him a woman bent over, resting her hands on her knees while her blond pony tail bounced to the rhythm of the horse's hoofbeats.

"There's something wrong in the left front ankle," the woman said.

"Hold up!" the man shouted to the rider.

The exercise boy eased the horse to a stop and walked the animal back toward the couple.

The man squatted down and felt the horse's ankle. "It's got heat in it. Take him back to the barn."

The exercise boy leaned down and spoke to the couple, who in unison turned to look at Laurel. "Could I help you?" the man asked.

Suddenly, Laurel felt very uncomfortable. She was fighting the urge to jump back in the truck and leave, but she composed herself, walked toward them and held out her hand. "I'm Laurel Mackenzie."

A smile spread across the woman's face. "Hello. I'm Karen Williams. I heard you speak at the Historical Society the other night. I really enjoyed it. This is my husband, Allen."

Allen Williams' big hand gripped Laurel's firmly. "Karen's done nothing but talk about you. She can't even keep her mind on the horses."

"She seems to have spotted that horse's problem," Laurel said.

"That she did," Williams said. "What brings you to Hickory Ridge, Miss Mackenzie? You gonna put something about racing in your next book?"

"I already have, Mr. Williams. I have another reason to be here. I've bought Belle Rouge and..." A shadow from behind her stopped Laurel in mid-sentence. This time, she recognized the voice.

"It seems we share another love, Miss Mackenzie. You're a racing enthusiast, too?"

"I've dreamed of racing a horse, Mr. Caulder."

"Then I'm sure Mr. Williams will be happy to accommodate you. If you'll excuse me now, I'll tend to my horse."

Laurel studied Lucien Caulder as he walked toward the barn and disappeared into the shadow of its interior. There was something in his manner that made her uneasy, but she had to admit she was attracted to him.

"That man gives me the creeps," Karen Williams said. "I wish he'd stayed at Churchill and never come out here."

"It's expensive to stable there. I don't think he has enough money," Allen replied.

"Does he have good horses?" Laurel asked.

"He used to have several, then his luck turned sour. He only has one in training now, but it's a good one, or it would be if he'd treat it right."

"Do you think he'd sell his horse?"

"You really are interested in getting into racing?"

"I might be, Mr. Williams, if I found the right horse. I don't have a lot of money."

"If you have the time, Miss Mackenzie, why don't you go into town with Karen and me and we'll have lunch. I have a deal you might be interested in."

Late on the next Friday afternoon, Eva and Jane went to Belle Rouge. They were waiting for Laurel to put on the last of her makeup, when Eva spoke. "Well, I never thought you'd ask to go to the sale barn again. I thought you didn't like flea markets."

"I'm not going to look at the booths. I'm going to the horse sale."

"Don't tell me you're going to buy a horse," Jane said.

"If I find the right one, I will. Allen said there's a dispersal of thoroughbreds tonight from a farm that's had some winners."

"How in the world are you going to take care of a horse with all you have to do?" Jane asked.

"Allen's made me a deal. If I let him keep two broodmares at Belle Rouge, he'll train a horse for me."

"You're going to be awfully busy," Eva said. "Are you sure you want to host the Historical Society's Christmas party at Belle Rouge?"

"Very certain. I want a good excuse to decorate the house. I know just the type of tree I want, and it's big, so I'll need some help. While we're at the sale barn, I'm going to look for that gentleman who sold me the furniture. He knew just what I wanted to make the old fireplace into a barbecue, so I'm sure he can find the perfect tree."

"Who is this Barney?" Jane asked.

"All I know about him is, he's fascinating to talk to and he's a good worker."

"I don't know anyone named 'Barney' in Cedarville. What's his last name?"

"I have no idea," Laurel replied. "I'll be ready as soon as I brush my hair."

"It's a little cool this evening," Eva said. "I think I'll go ahead and start the car. The heater will feel good."

As Eva walked across the back yard she saw to it that her path took her beside the barbecue. She paused only a moment to view the childlike printing in the concrete base. B-A-R-N-E-Y K., she read.

As their car turned into the parking lot of the sale barn, Laurel shook her head. "I can't believe people stand out here in this cold weather to sell this stuff."

"Some of these families have been coming here for years," Jane responded. "I guess it gets in their blood."

"Are you two going to the horse sale with me?" Laurel asked.

"Oh, we'll just look around. Maybe we can find Barney for you," Eva said.

Eva and Jane headed down one of the aisles between the booths. It was Eva who spoke first. "I don't think we're going to be able to find Barney."

"Why not?"

"Just a feeling I have, that's all. I did find out something when I went out to start the car. Barney signed his name in the concrete at the base of the barbecue. He put the letter 'K' for his last name."

Laurel made her way through the crowded doorway to the arena. She found a seat on the crude bleachers overlooking the small sale ring. As the horse sale began, the ring men hurried through one horse after another, of all sizes, shapes and conditions.

Laurel was relieved when she saw Allen and Karen Williams making their way toward her. "Sorry we're late," Allen apologized, "but we went out to the stabling area. I wanted to see what the dispersal consignment of horses looked like."

"I was hoping the first weren't the best," Laurel sighed.

"And now ladies and gentlemen," came the voice over the microphone, "the dispersal sale from the farm of Crit Sargent."

Laurel sat forward on her seat. "This is more like it."

They sat intently, watching the first few broodmares as they came through the ring. But Laurel's eyes did not brighten until a brilliant red mare was led in.

"Now folks," came the loud speaker again, "this is one of Crit's good mares...good breeding...old stock. Yes, she's got a little age on her...seventeen, the papers say, but folks...the vet verifies that she's in foal...due to drop around the first of March."

Laurel stood up. "I'll be back in a minute." She headed for the announcer's table and spoke to the auctioneer, who handed her the mare's registration papers.

Suddenly, she looked up at the Williamses, her mouth hanging open in surprise. Then she raised her hand on the opening bid of one thousand dollars. Quickly, the fifteen hundred bid came.

"Dammit!" Allen said, jumping to his feet. "They've spotted a newcomer. They'll take her to the cleaners if I don't get down there in a hurry."

Two thousand...twenty five... three thousand...the bidding climbed.

"They're running the price up on you. Back off!" Allen whispered in Laurel's ear.

"I've got three thousand from the lady here on my left. Do I hear thirty five?" From somewhere in the crowd there came the response. "Thirty five...do I hear four?"

"Wait, Laurel!" Allen commanded.

"Thirty five---do I hear four? Going once..."

"If you're determined to buy the mare, don't take the bid the auctioneer offers. Offer thirty seven-five."

"Going twice..."

"Thirty seven-five," Laurel echoed loudly.

"Thirty seven-five...do I heard four?"

"Four thousand," the auctioneer acknowledged.

"Walk away, Laurel."

"I want that mare!"

"Walk away like you're finished bidding!"

"She's a fine old mare," the voice of the auctioneer followed them. "Are there any more bids? Going once, going twice..."

"Forty two, Laurel. Bid forty two," Allen encouraged her.

"Forty two hundred! Going once...going twice...going three times. SOLD to the lady on my left."

"We did it Allen--I have a horse!"

"Ma'am...the lady who just bought the mare..." the voice came over the mike.

Laurel and Allen turned around to see two men trying to lead a young colt into the ring.

"Ma'am, you might be interested in this one, too. He's out of the mare you just bought."

The fiery red colt stood wide-eyed with fright, his head held high, his ears alert.

"He's coming two years of age---ready to break for the track," the auctioneer said.

"Laurel, you don't want him. Look at his right hoof. Look how it's turned in. Let's go."

But Allen Williams' words fell on deaf ears. Laurel was already headed back toward the announcer's table.

"Sir, that won't be no trouble to take care of," said an elderly black man leaning against the rail.

"Are you talking about that colt's hoof?" Allen asked.

"Yes sir. That colt's got heart. His leg don't matter. You're a good trainer. It won't be no problem at all. He's a fine horse."

Allen thought for a moment then made his way to Laurel's side. "The colt does look good. Go ahead and buy him. We'll give it a try."

Jane and Eva moved down the aisles of vendors, some of whom had put up tarpaulins as protection against the cold wind. "I'm freezing to death," Jane shivered. "There's no black man here selling anything and the man in the office said he hasn't seen anyone selling furniture who fits Barney's description. Let's find Laurel."

"There she is, coming out of the barn," Eva exclaimed.

"Look. She has some papers in her hand. Would you like to bet me she's bought a horse?"

"Hi, ladies," Karen greeted them. "Miss Mackenzie just got into the horse business."

"We knew she would," Eva sighed. "By the way, are you and Allen coming to the Christmas party Laurel's hosting at Belle Rouge?"

"We wouldn't miss it," Karen smiled again.

"Allen, did you choose the horse to buy?"

Laurel gave Allen no chance to answer. "I picked the mare and her colt. He's a good looking animal, isn't he, Allen?"

"Yes, he is. It probably won't make any difference about his leg."

"What's wrong with his leg?" Jane questioned.

"It just turns in a little bit," Laurel replied.

"Let me see those papers."

Laurel thrust the mare's registration papers toward Eva.

"Here's the main reason I bought them. Look at the mare's grandsire."

"I haven't the foggiest idea which is the grandsire."

"Right here," Laurel pointed.

Eva stared in disbelief. "Dear God---the name is Crimson Satan!"

## CHAPTER 6

Laurel studied the return address on the envelope. There was no doubt as to who sent the letter, but why now? she questioned. She ran her finger under the flap, broke the seal and unfolded the stationery to expose its hastily written contents.

*Mother,*

*I'm arriving on December 19. Hope it's OK if I spend Christmas vacation with you.*

*Beth*

Laurel frowned as she placed the note back into the envelope. "What's going on, Beth? You must want something. Why would you come here and not your father's for the holidays?" Her question was to remain unanswered, for she caught sight of Eva's car turning into the drive.

The dusty station wagon maneuvered through the stone gate posts and braked to a stop. Eva Farnsworth stared at the crimson maples standing stark and bare---black against the angry gray sky. She could never explain the strange feelings she often experienced, the same feelings she was experiencing at this moment. But she knew, each time she felt them something ominous was about to happen. Cautiously, she proceeded up the drive toward the mansion.

Laurel had done a remarkable job of restoring the place. The house was indeed beautiful. So why, Eva asked herself, did she feel a growing uneasiness each time she came to Belle Rouge. It was as if, with Laurel's restoration, the old farm was coming to life. She shuddered at the thought. There were too many ghosts here, too much sadness, but she knew there was nothing she could do to stop what was inevitable.

"Good morning," Laurel greeted her. "Barney found just the right tree for the foyer. Come on and see it. It will be glorious when it's decorated."

Laurel had placed box upon box of decorations at the base of the twelve-foot cedar and a ladder already stood in wait for them.

"This tree looks like it was made for the foyer," Eva exclaimed. "Just look at the way the staircase winds its way around it. I agree, it is perfect. Too bad Jane can't be here to decorate, but her cold has her under the weather."

Laurel picked up the first strand of lights. "Let's get started."

They wound the lights around the majestic tree and carefully hung each of the ornaments in its place. Finally, Laurel reached into the one remaining box of decorations. "It certainly is a good thing I found these, or we wouldn't have enough. They should just about top it off."

Eva lifted out a delicate ornament. "You said you found these?" she questioned.

"Yes, in a drawer of the antique chest I bought from Barney."

The ornament slipped from Eva's hand and crashed to the floor. "Oh, I'm sorry," she cried.

"No, don't worry about it. Let me see your finger. You've cut yourself. I'll get something for it."

Eva stood staring at broken glass on the floor. She stooped to pick up the pieces but instantly drew back her hand. She could not bring herself to touch it again.

Laurel returned with iodine and a band aid. "I'm sure there's no glass in the cut. It looks clean." She promptly finished her doctoring and then stopped to stare inquisitively at her patient. “Are you all right? You’re as pale as a ghost.”

“I’m fine, but maybe we could sit down for a minute.”

Laurel led her into the study. “I could call a doctor,” she offered.

“Don’t be silly. It’s a small cut. I’ll just rest for a bit.”

Eva sat back in the recliner, closed her eyes and waited until she felt her composure return. When at last she opened her eyes, she found Laurel staring at her again. “Nothing’s wrong,” Eva assured her. “I was just collecting myself. Let’s finish the decorating.”

Eva held the ladder and watched as Laurel adjusted the star on top of the tree. “Tell me again where you got these old ornaments,” she said.

“In the dresser I bought from Barney. You don’t suppose they could have belonged to the Kilgores, do you? Wouldn’t that be remarkable?”

“Most remarkable,” Eva agreed.

“I’ve fixed some lunch for us. I’m sure you’ll feel much better after you eat.”

“Will you?” Eva asked.

“Eva Farnsworth! It’s a little disconcerting when you’re continuously reading my mind. But, I guess there’s no use trying to hide anything from you. You’re right. There is something bothering me. My daughter’s coming here for Christmas vacation.”

“I should think that would make you happy.”

“More curious than anything. There’s usually an ulterior motive when she wants to see me.”

“Why don’t you give her the benefit of the doubt? Maybe it will be different this time. What else is bothering you?”

"You're something else," Laurel smiled. "It's just that I had an invitation this morning. Lucien Caulder phoned. He asked me to dinner. I don't know if I should go. What do you think?"

"It's not my decision. Why ask me?"

"I don't know. I have this little feeling."

"I usually go with my gut feelings," Eva replied.

"I'm just being silly. I do know what's wrong with me. I've not been asked out on a date since I've been divorced. I'm scared."

The sound of crunching gravel on the drive leading to the barn prevented Eva's reply. Allen Williams' truck and van were making the delivery of his broodmares. Karen Williams waved to them as she opened the gate.

Laurel reached for her jacket. "Come on. Let's see what horses they've brought."

"You go ahead and I'll take care of the dishes," Eva said.

Karen Williams untied the mares through the front window of the trailer, while her husband let the tailgate down. First one and then the other horse moved backward down the ramp until it found steady footing on the ground. Laurel eagerly took the lead shank of the black mare and followed Allen, who led a small bay into the pasture, where they turned them loose.

The two newcomers were welcomed with a snort and a challenge by Laurel's red mare. The bay pinned back her ears and wheeled to kick. The black danced menacingly with neck arched. Suddenly, Laurel's mare bared her teeth and lunged, and both of the Williams' mares turned and fled at a gallop.

"Flame! Flame!" Laurel called. "Whoa, girl!"

"Don't worry," Allen laughed. "Your mare's just showing them who's boss." Soon the three horses settled into grazing.

"Laurel, would you mind if I went to the house and washed my hands?" Karen asked.

"Go right ahead, Eva's there. And would you ask her to make some coffee?"

Laurel waited until Karen disappeared into the house before she spoke again. "Your wife's a hard worker. You're fortunate to have someone who enjoys the same things you do."

"I know that," Allen agreed. "She's a big help. Say, when are you coming to the training center to see your colt? We're going to put him out on the track soon."

"I never dreamed he'd be ready this quickly."

"He's taken right to the training, acts as though he likes it."

"I'll be there in a day or two. Let's go in, I'm freezing."

Eva was pouring four steaming cups of coffee when Allen and Laurel entered the kitchen. "Are you still planning on coming to the Christmas party here at Belle Rouge?" she asked the Williams.

"You bet," Karen answered. "This is a great house for a party. Is it true that it's haunted?"

"Maybe Laurel should have had a Halloween party," Eva laughed uneasily.

Karen persisted. "Are there any ghosts?"

"Don't start on that stuff," Allen chided. "We have to get going. We've got a horse in the tenth race tomorrow at Churchill. Would you two ladies like to come? It's the last day of the racing season. I have some extra passes."

"Not in this weather," Eva shivered.

"I'd love to go, but I have a dinner engagement," Laurel answered. "Maybe next time."

After the Williams left, Laurel found time to ask a question that had been on her mind for some time. "Do you think Claire could have kept a diary like her mother did?"

"I think it's possible," Eva said, "especially since we believe she may have written that bizarre last entry in Lily's."

"Could it also be hidden on this property?"

"It could be, but where would you look?"

"Someplace where no one would think of looking." Laurel frowned. "I have a feeling---just a hunch---that if Claire had a diary, she, or someone, didn't want it found."

"I agree with you. There were secrets being kept about the Kilgores, and I think my great-grandfather was helping to keep them."

"I have to know what the secrets are."

"Maybe some things are best left alone."

"I can't stand not knowing," Laurel declared.

"Yes, I know," Eva sighed. "I'm having the same problem."

"May I come to your house again, soon?" Laurel asked. "I didn't get a chance to see Doctor James' record book. Maybe the two of us can piece this puzzle together."

Eva had just left when Lucien Caulder phoned. Laurel hesitated for a moment before she accepted his extended offer. But why shouldn't she go with him to Churchill Downs and then have dinner, she told herself. She did want to see Allen Williams' horse run.

Laurel replaced the receiver and sat for a moment, staring at the phone. Then she pulled her legs up tightly against her chest and rested her head on her knees. "I want to go with him, but I can't understand why he unnerves me."

Abruptly, she unfolded herself and sprang to her feet. "It's so silly to think I could be attracted to him. I hardly know him." Her pacing brought her to the huge window in the front room. She pulled back the heavy green drapes and peered through the antique lace curtain. The bare crimson maples were just disappearing into the coming darkness. She turned away to find herself melting into the shadows of the old house.

"I wonder what it would be like to be with him," she questioned. Quickly, she admonished herself. "Would you listen to me? I certainly don't need that. I enjoy my freedom. I don't need to complicate my life again."

At noon the next day, Laurel was once again pacing the floor. Intermittently, she glanced at her watch, then peered out the window. "I know he said he'd be here at twelve and here it is, twelve thirty. Surely I didn't misunderstand him."

Then without warning, the knock came at the front door. Laurel swallowed and took a deep breath. Don't appear too eager, she told herself. Her hand trembled slightly as she turned the knob.

The years had been graciously kind to Lucien Caulder. The only a hint of gray in his black curly hair was at his temples. The few lines in his face only accented his rugged good looks. His black eyes dominated his features. They were, Laurel knew, sometimes brooding, but most often they were piercing, never wavering---seemingly offering a challenge to any potential enemy.

On the way to Churchill Downs, he did not mention his tardiness and neither did she. Laurel had to admit to herself that she was afraid he wouldn't come. As she sat next to him, she could not help but wonder what it would feel like to be touched by him.

The owner's sticker on the windshield of Lucien's car allowed them to park close to the Club House entrance. He made no attempt to open the car door for her. She fumbled for the handle and by the time she got the door open he was already twenty feet ahead of her. When she caught up with him at the gate, he was handing the ticket taker two passes.

Lucien did not offer her his arm to help her navigate the brick walkway, so she slipped her arm through his. For an instant, she thought he would pull away, but he slowed his gait to match hers.

Laurel had never been to the historic track before, and she craned her neck to study the immense wooden structure. Long rows of pari-mutuel windows lined the old walkway that lay the same as it must have over a hundred years ago. Only the blare of television sets hanging from the girders kept one aware that it was the twentieth century at Churchill Downs. It was not until the patio area was reached that the Downs moved completely into the modern day. The new paddock stood bright and gleaming beneath a tote board topped by a huge television screen.

They stopped in the center of the patio, where Laurel could see---over the multiple entrances into the cavernous grandstand---the names of the Kentucky Derby winners, most painted in white, but some glistening gold in the sunlight.

"Triple Crown winners are in gold," Lucien's voice broke her thoughts.

"Am I that transparent?" she asked. "I thought Eva Farnsworth was the only one who could read my mind."

She had hoped a smile could be found on Lucien's face, but he opened the racing form. Laurel noticed he had obviously been studying it carefully. Certain horses' names were circled and others marked out.

"You can get a program over there," Lucien motioned toward a booth. "Get me one, too."

Laurel handed the money to the vender, who in turn gave her two programs. When she offered Lucien one, he took it without looking up from the form. He then led the way back under the grandstand, down one of the side walkways and out toward a box seat next to the rail. How good it felt to take advantage of the warmth of the sun on this chilly, late November day, Laurel thought.

This was Laurel Mackenzie's dream come true. She could hardly believe she was finally here at Churchill Downs. Since she could remember, the first Saturday in May had found her sitting in front of the TV, voraciously devouring every bit of the commentary on the Kentucky Derby. It was during the first stretch call she ever saw that she secretly vowed she would one day come to the Downs and watch a horse carry her colors to victory. Even the thought of watching Allen's horse held such joy for her.

She glanced at the handsome man next to her. She wondered what it would be like to share her dream with him as Karen did with Allen. Could Lucien Caulder be the one missing piece that would make her life complete?

As the race card progressed, Laurel could not help but see Lucien's roll of money grow larger. "You're doing much better than I," she said. For the first time, Laurel saw an engaging smile cross his face.

He leaned close to her and his dark eyes seemed to soften. "Maybe you should listen to me all the time," he said.

Laurel could feel his warm breath against her cheek. His arm was around her shoulders and she responded as he, ever so gently, pulled her closer to him. She so wanted to kiss him, but suddenly, he pulled away and turned his attention to the feature race. "Have you studied your program?" he asked.

"Not this race," she replied. Quickly her eyes scanned the list of the horses' names. "Is there something special? I don't see..." Just then something caught her eye. "The number eight horse is out of a Crimson Satan mare," she smiled.

"And what else?" Lucien smiled.

"It's the favorite. And the owner is---Lucien Caulder! Your horse is running and you didn't tell me? How exciting! And you've done quite well with him. He has a pretty good record."

"More than pretty good", Lucien stated. "Mystic Warrior has the best record of any horse in the race."

"Oh, I agree. It's amazing he could maintain a record like this, especially since he runs so often." Laurel knew she had said the wrong thing the moment the words left her mouth. She knew better than to try to make amends as she watched him withdraw like some wounded animal.

"I'm going to the paddock," he said abruptly. "You coming?"

Laurel followed him back beneath the stands and across the courtyard. He did not invite her into the ring, so she stood watching as the horses were being led in.

One by one the horses entered, some going directly into the saddling enclosure, some taking a turn walking around the ring. It was indeed a good looking field of horses---bays, bright chestnuts, dark browns, all dappled, their strong muscles rippling. No horse was led into the number eight stall until the last one entered the ring. The handler led the colt one lap around. Its coat, unlike the rest, was dull, as if burned by too much exposure to the sun. The horse's mane hung, slightly disheveled, and its step was slow and methodical. Just as the horse passed Laurel, it turned its head and looked directly at her. Its eyes were not alert, but something shone through them. Perhaps it was grit and determination, but Laurel felt it must be what horsemen call "heart".

Instead of returning to the box seat, Lucien stopped in front of a television screen beneath the grandstand. Anxiously, he watched the parade to the post, all the while twisting the program in his hands.

The horses loaded into the gate with no problem and immediately upon the sound of the bell, the animals catapulted forward. In just a few jumps, Mystic Warrior had the lead. The rest of the pack would have to catch him. Fractions of 22 flat for the first quarter and 45:2 for the half were registered. By the time 1:11 for the six furlongs was flashed on the screen, the horses were rounding the turn, heading down the long stretch toward the finish line. Mystic Warrior's five length lead was being eaten away. At the eighth pole, the gallant colt seemed to bobble. By the time they reached the sixteenth pole, the colt was fighting, struggling to hold on, but one by one four horses passed him.

Lucien whalloped his folded program against the bench. "That son of a bitch!" he seethed. "I'll show him what happens to a quitter."

As they ate dinner, Laurel could see that Lucien's anger was being replaced by something else. She could feel his desire for her growing. Unabashedly, his eyes followed her every movement. It was as if he were performing some animalistic ritual, some silent communication, questioning, propositioning. She knew what her reply would be.

When they entered the mansion at Belle Rouge, she did not reach for the light. She led him down the hallway and into her bedroom. The moon, its rays streaming through the aged windows panes, formed an intricate pattern of frail light across the bed.

Hastily, they undressed. She could feel his hot breath on her neck. His hands were not soft and gentle as she had imagined, but hard and groping. He pressed her down onto the bed and forced her legs apart.

The image of some wild mountain cat crossed her mind---a cat bent on satisfying its voracious appetite---tearing at its victim's flesh, reducing it to helplessness.

He lay, heaving, on top of her for a moment, energy spent, nostrils sucking in his body's desperate need for air.

Laurel reached up and smoothed back his hair from his forehead. Her hands caressed his muscular shoulders. She moved her body under his, seeking the satisfaction that had eluded her. Quickly he rose to his hands and knees, left a brief kiss on her cheek and reached for his clothes.

"Don't get up. I'll see myself out." He paused in the doorway. "I'll call."

Laurel heard the car motor start on the second try. Stiffly, she got up, her body already beginning to ache. She watched out the window as Lucien's car sped down the driveway.

She didn't bother to search for her nightgown, instead she pulled back the cover and fell into bed. The stinging pain was growing inside her body, but she smiled as she closed her eyes. It had been a long time since she had felt so desired.

## CHAPTER 7

Lucien Caulder became a daily visitor to Belle Rouge. Laurel shared with him her hopes and desires for restoring the farm. The barn would be her next project. She planned to redo the stalls, saving as much of the original wood as possible, and she wanted to build a new staircase to the loft. Lucien took special interest in the furniture she had purchased from Barney. Laurel had even pointed out the Christmas ornaments she had found. It was not until Lucien asked to go up into the glass room that she hesitated.

"It's been nailed shut," she told him.

"I really do want to see the view from there," he persisted.

There was a small part of Laurel that wanted to stand firm against him, but she knew she could not. She wondered why she so wanted to please him. Then she realized the answer--she was afraid she might lose him if she didn't.

She followed him up the steps. He had already reached the glass room when she stopped and looked up toward him. He extended his hand to her, but she was suddenly reluctant to touch him. Looming above her, he reminded Laurel of a huge black bird ready to attack its prey. She closed her eyes and took a deep breath. Her fear was not of him, she told herself, it was only the glass room.

Something made her look back down the steps. Maybe it was a flash of color---perhaps it was a movement. Then she saw her. Claire Kilgore stood in the hallway beneath them. Laurel heard her speak.

"Everything will be all right, Ross. You'll see. Daddy will forgive you. When Satan wins the Gold Cup, he'll forget about the mare. It wasn't your fault she died."

"But it was my fault. I should have kept a closer eye on her. I just didn't realize it was that close to her foaling time. Now Father despises me. He told me I am too irresponsible to ever inherit Belle Rouge. He's going to leave the farm to you, Claire."

"Even if he does, this will always be your home," she soothed him. "You will never have to worry about that."

Lily Kilgore listened from the doorway, her eyes blazing with an unaccustomed anger. "That man will pay for this," she seethed.

"No, Mamma, please don't say anything to Daddy," Claire begged. "Please!"

As Lily turned to go, she found the massive form of Sumner Kilgore blocking her way.

"Say anything to me about what?" he demanded.

"You beast!" Lily lunged at her husband with clenched fists. "How dare you treat your son this way---threatening to disown him."

Sumner grabbed her wrists and held her at arms length. "No son of mine would be here in the house whimpering behind his mother's skirts. He'd be at the barn wanting to ride the next Gold Cup winner."

"Father, please," Ross begged. "Let Mother go. I'll ride Satan. I can do it. I know I can."

Kilgore relaxed his grip on his wife. "You really want to do that?" he smiled.

"Yes, I want to."

"Sumner, no," Lily pleaded. "Don't let Ross get on that animal."

"He's twenty years old, woman. He can make up his own mind. If he wants to ride Satan, he can. You would have him do nothing but stay in this house and paint those infernal pictures."

"But painting is what he loves to do."

"No! You're not going to coddle him anymore. It's time he became a man."

"Come on up here." Lucien's voice drew Laurel back. "You aren't afraid of heights, are you?"

"No. Of course, I'm not," she said, placing her hand in his. She stepped into the glass room, aware that she had begun to tremble.

They stood together, Lucien behind her, his arms around her waist, his breath on her cheek. Laurel relaxed, closed her eyes and leaned back against him. When she opened them, she saw the figures again---this time on the path below. Lily Kilgore was following her husband, who was hastily making his way toward the stable.

"Let your daughter ride the horses," Lily begged. "Claire's the one who loves them, not Ross."

Kilgore stopped abruptly and wheeled about to face her. "My daughter is only fifteen years old and she can ride anything in the barn."

"She's so much like you," Lily cried. "Isn't one child enough for you to have? Please don't take my son away from me."

"Ross asked me to let him ride Satan."

Lily clutched her husband's arm. "He's just doing it because he thinks that's what you want!"

"Let it be," Sumner demanded. "Ross is going to give Satan his workout this morning."

"No, no!" Lily screamed.

"That's right," he called after her. "Run away. Run to that cursed observatory and hide. Ross will ride this horse and you can't do anything about it!"

"Laurel. Laurel! What's wrong?" Lucien questioned.

"Nothing. I just want to go downstairs."

She asked him to stay the night and they made love. But afterward, Laurel lay awake, her thoughts refusing to give way to anything but dozing. When Lucien's deep, rhythmic breathing assured her he was sound asleep, she got out of bed and made her way down the hall to the study. She closed the door and began to write.

*Claire was waiting for her mother when she reached the house. "Momma, what did Daddy say? Will he stop Ross from riding?"*

*"Your father's going to kill your brother," Lily sobbed. "Claire, go stop Ross! He'll listen to you."*

*"Lie down and rest, Momma. I'll take care of everything."*

*Ross was already pulling on his boots by the time Claire got to his room. "Please. You can't do this," she said. "Satan is too hard to handle."*

*"I have to. Nothing I've ever done has pleased my father. He hates my painting, and he hates me."*

*"I'll ask him for the money to send you to school in Paris."*

*"You've already asked him once and he became furious. I won't let you do it again. Maybe Father's right, maybe it's time I tried to be what he wants me to be."*

*As Ross left his room, he passed his mother in the hallway. "Please, don't," she pleaded. "I know something terrible is going to happen."*

*Ross grabbed a riding crop that lay on the hall tree. "Mother, I can't take this anymore. You and Father have me in a tug of war. I would like to do what you want of me, but my father is so much stronger."*

*Claire started to follow her brother down the stairs, but the cry that escaped from her mother's throat made her stop in her tracks. It was a wail not unlike that of a mortally wounded animal. "Mother, please don't go up there! Please don't go into the glass room!"*

Suddenly, Laurel was aware of a figure beside her. She screamed as the hands gripped her shoulders. Wildly she flailed about trying to avoid the arms that were closing round her---immobilizing her. "Let me go!" she cried, but a hand clamped over her mouth.

"Laurel! Stop it! It's Lucien. For god's sake, stop it!"

She felt her body relax and he removed his hand from over her mouth. "Lucien, you almost scared me to death. Why did you come up behind me like that?"

"I woke up and you were gone. Then I heard the typewriter. What in the world are you doing this time of night?"

"I'm writing. I got an idea for the next chapter in my book, so I'm getting it down before I forget it."

"You'd better start getting those ideas during the daytime. I won't want my night's sleep interrupted after we're married."

It was the startled look on Laurel's face that made him continue. "You can't tell me you haven't thought about it. We have a lot in common--- our love for history--- horses---this farm.

In an instant, Laurel could hear herself speaking, but it was as if it were someone else's voice. The voice stated that she was not ready for a step as big as marriage. Hastily, she explained that yesterday she had talked to her daughter on the phone. "Beth is very upset. She found out her father is going to remarry. That's why she wants to come to Kentucky for the holidays. She's feeling abandoned by her father. I can't abandon her, too," the voice concluded. "At least not now."

The expression on Lucien's face did not escape Laurel. "I didn't realize you had a daughter," he said. "You've never mentioned her."

"We've not been close. She adores her father. This is the first move she's made toward me in a long time. I can't pass up this opportunity. But you'll like Beth. I want you two to become friends. I'm sure she'll like you."

Lucien led her back into the bedroom. "Yes, I'm sure I'll like her." He undid Laurel's robe, then picked her up and carried her to the bed. "She'll like me as much as her mother does," he smiled.

A night of restless sleep had brought Eva Farnsworth to her Victorian parlor sometime after midnight. She had lighted the various colored and shaped candles in the room, hoping to find some comfort in their glow.

She did not remember if she had fallen asleep on the couch or simply placed herself in a meditative state, but whatever happened, she felt rested now as she watched the morning's sun rise.

She blew out what remained of the candles and recalled the cause of the night's concern. When she retired, her mind had been filled with thoughts of Laurel Mackenzie. What really led her to Cedarville, she wondered?

Eva didn't believe in mere coincidence, she believed the Supreme Being had more of a plan for his creations than that. It was almost as if a 'gathering' of people was taking place around Laurel. There was Barney, the woman on the plane, and even herself. She shuddered at the thought, but it was as if the inhabitants of Belle Rouge, Doctor Timothy James, Preston Miller, and Alexandra Lennox were gathering too.

Eva had never been afraid of ghosts, or beings---whatever people chose to call the phenomenon she preferred to call, "energies." But she was frightened last night. Even in the light of morning, the mere thought of one other disturbing question made a cold chill run the length of her spine. What was Lucien Caulder's part in all this?

She had just poured herself a cup of coffee when Jane's call came. "I've had another one of my dreams. I know it's early, but may I come over?"

Eva was waiting on the porch for her when she pulled in the driveway. "I'm glad you called, Jane. I was about to phone you. It seems as though last night was disturbing for both of us. Sit down and tell me your dream."

Dreams came frequently to Jane. Often she could recall them in minute detail. As far as she could analyze them, they fell in three categories: Some simply provided clarification as to what her sub-conscious held; some aided in the understanding of situations in her life and, oftentimes, those of her friends; the final type of dream afforded her a look into the future. But last night's dream was different. It gave her a glimpse into the past.

Jane began. "I saw my great-grandfather Preston Miller. He was in Louisville for a meeting with Alexandra Lennox."

Preston Miller's boots clicked across the marble floor of the lobby of the Lennox Hotel. Suddenly, he felt terribly out of place. He straightened his leather jacket, pulling it together over his homespun shirt.

The clerk at the desk eyed him with suspicion. "Yes?" came his curt greeting.

Miller's eyes narrowed and the thin, precisely dressed clerk raised one eyebrow. "Well, what do you want?" the man asked impatiently.

"A little courtesy would be good for a start," Miller replied.

The clerk jerked his head as if he had been struck by some unseen hand. "Sir, we are the finest hotel in the city, the state and perhaps the country. We are known for our courtesy to an elite clientele. Now if you are looking for a room, perhaps the City Hotel would be more to your liking."

Preston Miller reached across the desk and pulled the wiry little man's face close to his. "What is to my liking, you little bastard, is to knock your head off."

Alexandra Lennox entered the lobby just in time to hear the exchange of words. "Andre, is there a problem?" she asked.

"Yes, Mrs. Lennox," the clerk squeaked as he tried to catch his breath. "I was just about to call security and have this man ejected."

"Why would you do that to my personal guest?" Alexandra asked. "I think you were very rude to him. He's due an apology."

"Ma'am, I'm sorry. I didn't know he was your friend."

"And Andre---I want to correct something you said to Sheriff Miller. We are not a hotel catering to the elite. We are an elite hotel because we cater to the wishes of ALL our guests. Since you do not appear to hold with that philosophy, I suggest you gather your things. I'll find a clerk who does."

"No, Mrs. Lennox," Preston Miller interrupted. "That won't be necessary. I believe Andre now understands your policy, which I might add, is a fine one, very similar to the one I follow at my hotel. You probably shouldn't fire Andre. I'd hire him in a minute. I'm sure he would upgrade the Cedarville Hotel and then it would become elite. It might even rival the Lennox."

Alexandra held her breath, desperately trying to stifle a giggle. She took the sheriff's arm and guided him toward the staircase. "Andre, see to it we're not disturbed," she called back over her shoulder.

"Yes ma'am," the wide-eyed clerk quickly responded.

It was not until they rounded the circle in the staircase that Alexandra turned to face the sheriff. "You big lummox!" she scolded him. "I thought I would burst when you said you'd hire Andre."

Preston Miller let go a mighty roar of laughter. "Can you imagine him standing behind the desk of the Cedarville Hotel? He would scare my clientele to death."

"Oh, you don't know how good it feels to laugh," Alexandra sighed. "There's not been much to laugh about lately."

"No ma'am, not if you're referring to the Kilgores." "How is Lily?"

"Dr. James is worried about her."

Alexandra studied Miller's face. She wondered if he knew the truth.

"Is that all?" Eva asked. "No explanation as to what 'the truth' meant?"

"None," Jane replied. "But it had to do with Timothy James."

"Come into the parlor. I want to read you something Doctor James wrote in his diary."

Eva found the page.

*I cannot help but believe someone has been administering some sort of a drug to Lily Kilgore other than the one I prescribed. I find her moods have become too changeable, too extreme. Only one person in the house would have had the opportunity or the motive to do such a deed. Gen.*

"Who is Gen?" Jane asked.

"I don't know. My great-grandfather mentions her several times in his writings."

"Have you told Laurel how Lily died?"

"No. I thought she would be back here by now, wanting to read the record book."

"She may have been too busy. I called Karen Williams last night to ask her what dish she was bringing to the Christmas party at Belle Rouge. She gave me a little more information than I asked for. Laurel's been seeing Lucien Caulder. Karen thinks the relationship may be getting serious."

"Oh dear," Eva sighed. "You know that man better than I do. What's he up to?"

"Whatever it is, you can bet it has to do with money," Jane replied.

Laurel awoke with a start to find that Lucien was not beside her. She put on her robe and proceeded to the kitchen.

The coffee was made and his car was still in the drive behind the house. He had mentioned that he would like to walk over the pasture. Perhaps that's where he was, she thought.

She took her cup of coffee into the study and sat down to read what she had typed during the night, before Lucien had interrupted her. "Not bad," she said to herself. "In fact, it's very good. But where do I go from here?" The image of the glass-room appeared in her mind. "I'm not going there again," she said aloud.

Laurel sat for a while, desperately searching her mind for the words, but her fingers only rested on the typewriter keys. It was as if her mind were blank. "All right. I'll go," she said. "I didn't faint the last time I went up there. I'll be fine. And I have to know what happened to Ross."

Laurel went up to the second floor. "Jane's correct," she thought. "This room is too small, compared to the others. And it should have a window in it. She ran her hand over what appeared to be the outside wall. "The window's not covered over."

Then she made a fist and rapped across part of it. "Damn, it's hollow. Someone has added this wall."

"OK," she said to herself, "I know I'm stalling. I'm going to the observatory now." She gave the wall one last look, then questioned again. "But why did they leave no opening in it?"

Laurel's question went unanswered, for there was a sound coming from the hall. It began as a moan, then soon escalated to a high pitched frenzy, only to ease into a whimper.

Laurel could hear her own heart as it began to pound. Carefully, she made her way to the door leading into the hall and peered around the corner. This time the sound came as a wail. The trap door leading into the glass room moved ever so slightly as the cry reached its zenith. "The wind!" Laurel sighed in relief. "It's only the wind."

She climbed the steps and unlocked the door. When she lifted it, it felt as if the room released a deep sigh. Laurel pushed with all her might, and the door gave way and fell back against the floor of the observatory. "It's only the wind," she reassured herself.

The panes of glass were beginning to cloud with the approaching cold front, but Laurel could see the figures below. The black jockey was giving Ross Kilgore a leg up on Red Satan.

"Give him his head!" Sumner Kilgore exclaimed. "Let's see just how fast this devil can run!"

The red stallion reared and lunged forward. Ross momentarily lost his balance and grabbed for the horse's mane.

"Hang on son, you can do it. Don't let 'em get the best of you!"

Claire relaxed when she saw her brother settle his weight on the saddle. "Come on Ross, you can do it," she called. "Hold him steady and he'll be all right. Satan, you devil, run straight," she said under her breath. "Don't you dare try any of your tricks."

All seemed to be going well until the horse and rider rounded the turn into the backstretch. Then, Claire remembered something she had seen.

"Daddy! Ross is carrying a whip! Did you tell him not to use it?"

A look of horror crossed Sumner Kilgore's face.

Claire bounded over the fence just as Ross drew the whip from under his arm. "Ross stop! Don't hit him!"

As the whip came down on the horse's side, Red Satan vaulted and Ross lost his grip on the mane and the reins.

Claire stopped abruptly. Her brother was sliding sideways in the saddle. She could only pray he would fall free of the horse's slashing hooves. She watched in terror as Ross's boot became entangled in the stirrup.

Frantically, he attempted to free himself, but by now, Satan was in a panic. The horse sprinted down the straightaway, trying desperately to rid himself of the struggling rider. Ross's body went limp. He was being dragged down the track and it became apparent there was no way to stop the frightened animal.

Satan moved toward the inside rail and Ross's head hit first one post and then another and another. Finally, the stallion stopped at the gate to the barn. Claire started toward the lifeless form dangling from the stirrup, but Barnabas blocked her way. "Don't look, Missy. You don't wanna see."

"But I must help my brother!"

The black man's voice was firm. "Miss Claire, you know as well as I do, there's nothin' we can do for Mr. Ross now."

She offered no resistance when Barnabas took her arm and led her up the path toward the house. Halfway there, she stopped and turned around to see the stable hands lowering Ross's body to the ground.

Sumner Kilgore took Satan's reins and tied him to a post. Methodically, he took his pistol from its holster and slowly raised his arm till it was level with the head of the unsuspecting animal.

The shot rang out, followed immediately by an all too familiar wail from the third-floor observatory. When Claire looked up, she saw her mother beating her fists on the panes of glass. Suddenly, the entire wall shattered under the punishment and Lily Kilgore stepped upon the window sill.

Laurel could feel some unseen force pushing her. She was standing on the window sill.

"Get back! Get away from the edge," she heard a voice.

Instinctively, she reached for the side wall of glass. It was enough to steady her footing, and she held on, unable to move for what seemed an eternity. Then she felt someone easing her back off the ledge and onto the floor.

Eva held her tightly. "Dear God, what were you doing on the ledge?"

"I don't know," Laurel sobbed. "I was just standing here, looking toward the race track. Oh Eva, it was horrible. I saw Red Satan kill Ross. Then I felt something pushing me toward the glass. It broke. I was standing on the ledge. Then I heard...it was you. I heard your voice. You were down in the garden. You yelled at me to get back."

"Oh, look at your hands and arms," Eva said. "You're bleeding. We've got to get you to the doctor."

"What's happening to me?" Laurel sobbed. "Am I losing my mind?"

## CHAPTER 8

Laurel thought the doctor believed her story. She told him she was standing on a ladder, washing a window and fell, cutting her arms. She was sure Eva knew she lied about what happened, but Laurel also realized her friend had not been altogether truthful with her. Eva knew more than she let on about the happenings at Belle Rouge. Somehow Laurel would pry the information from her.

Eva drove Laurel's car out of the doctor's parking lot and onto the main street. "Why don't we stop by your house?" Laurel said. "I want to read your great-grandfather's writings."

Soon Laurel was seated on the couch in Eva's parlor, holding Doctor James' record book. Her face contorted into a curious frown.

"Is something bothering you?" Eva asked.

"It's this book," Laurel replied. "When I took it from you, I felt something. I felt as though a part of a puzzle were being put into place."

"I think it is," Eva agreed. "Read this entry."

*I cannot believe Lily would destroy herself in such a manner as to jump from the observatory atop the Belle Rouge mansion. Even though she witnessed Ross's death, I do not believe--- I will never believe--- it was in her nature to commit suicide.*

Laurel closed the book and laid it on the couch beside her. "Please, Eva. Help me understand what happened to me today in that glass room."

Eva sat back in the rocking chair and closed her eyes for a moment. Laurel recognized the look on her face. It was the same look she had when she was resting at Belle Rouge after breaking the Christmas ornament. Laurel waited patiently for her to speak.

Finally, Eva began. "It's not possible for me to put all my beliefs into just a few statements. But I will share this one with you. I hope you can remain open-minded. I believe it's possible for us to step into someone else's energy."

"Like stepping into their space?" Laurel asked. "My daughter uses that phrase all the time."

"For me, it's more than that. I think it is possible for people's energy to remain on earth, even when they are no longer living."

"Why would their energy remain?" Laurel questioned.

"Perhaps they have unfinished business."

"You believe Lily Kilgore has some unfinished business?"

"I think it's possible," Eva replied.

"Why me? Why have I stepped into her energy?"

"It may be nothing more than the fact you live in her house."

"What can her unfinished business be?"

"If we had the answer to that, we'd better understand what's going on."

"O-o-h," Laurel shuddered. "You make her seem alive."

"I'm going to offer a suggestion," Eva said. "You may want to have the glass room torn down."

"No! I would never do that."

"But you hate that room. Jane and I had to practically force you to go up there. Why are you so determined to keep it now?"

"It can't be torn down."

"Why, Laurel? Be honest with me. Tell me why."

"Because---because---that's where I'm getting the story for my new book. It comes to me when I'm in there."

"Is that the only place it comes to you?"

"Yes. That's the only place."

"You aren't telling the whole truth," Eva said. "You don't have to lie to me."

Laurel looked away. "When I'm with Lucien," she said. "I feel the story when I'm with Lucien."

Eva kept herself from making any comment. She simply said, "Thank you. We no longer have any need to keep secrets from one another. And you're right about this being a puzzle. I believe several people hold various pieces. I phoned Jane when you were in the doctor's office. She should be here soon. I want her to relate her dream to you."

It was noon by the time Jane arrived. While they ate the sandwiches Eva had prepared, she told Laurel of the dream about Preston Miller and Alexandra Lennox.

The women were back in the parlor when Eva again took her great-grandfather's record book from the shelf. She read aloud the first passage containing the name 'Gen.' "Who in the world is this person?" she asked.

"The black jockey's wife," Laurel answered.

"How do you know that?"

"Do you remember when the three of us went into the glass room? I saw Gen that day. I heard the jockey call her name. I didn't remember it till now."

"All right," Eva said, "here's what we'll do from now on. Jane, when you dream, relate everything to us, no matter how unimportant it may seem. Laurel, when you see these 'energies' at Belle Rouge, tell us everything. And I will go over Doctor James's book once again. There may be something I've missed."

"Oh! I just remembered something else," Laurel exclaimed. "Lucien was at Belle Rouge this morning. He must be wondering what happened to me."

"I didn't see him," Eva said.

"But you must have seen his car. It was parked at the side of the house."

"I parked in the circle out front. The door was standing ajar, so I walked through the house thinking I'd find you. When you weren't there, I went out the back door. I guess I could have missed seeing his car. Where was he while you were in the glass room?"

"He said something about walking over the back field. I think I'd better phone him."

"Use the extension in the kitchen," Eva suggested.

When Laurel left the parlor, Jane asked a question. "Should I tell her what we discussed?"

"Yes," Eva replied. "We must not keep secrets any longer."

After a few minutes, Laurel returned and plopped back down on the couch. "He doesn't answer. I'll try again a little later."

"There's something I need to tell you," Jane said. "But I'm not sure how you'll take it."

"Please, go ahead," Laurel responded. "I want to know everything."

"Just remember, this happened several years ago. And I don't want you to think I'm meddling in your business, but---at one time, Lucien Caulder and I were engaged."

"Go on," Laurel urged, hiding her surprise.

"I broke off the engagement, because it became apparent that Lucien had a dark side to his personality. The first time I saw it was one day when we were riding in my car. I said something he didn't like and he grabbed me by my hair and pulled so hard I almost lost control of the car. I was so stunned I couldn't say anything."

"Then a second incident happened. I've never told this to a soul, not even Eva. It was late one afternoon and I was fixing supper at his house. Without warning, he picked me up, carried me to the bed, and tried to---and tried to rape me. I fought him off. I thought for an instant that he might hit me, but instead he got up and went to the kitchen. When I entered the room, he was standing at the sink. I went over to him, wanting to discuss what had just happened. I wanted to tell him that I would have sex with him but not in that manner. He stepped away from me and picked up a butcher knife. He stood there, smiling, as he flicked his thumb across the blade."

"I knew I had to call his bluff. 'You even try to use that,' I said, 'and you'll live to regret it.' My boldness must have startled him, because he laid the knife down. I left, and I never set foot in his house again."

Laurel stood up. "Eva, maybe Jane will drive you to Belle Rouge to get your car. I need to take care of some business."

Laurel didn't know the exact location of Lucien's house, but she knew which road. It shouldn't be hard to find. It was on a rural route and she surmised that his name would be on the mailbox. She drove to the end of the road, but no mailbox could be found. She was about halfway back to Cedarville when she recognized his car in the drive of a small, gray house. It was not the type of home she expected for Lucien Caulder.

When she turned in, she spotted him in the back yard. He was walking toward a hound chained in front of a dog house. The animal yelped, then lunged for the plate of food Lucien carried in his hand. Lucien landed a kick on the dog's ribs and it ducked its tail and crept into its house. It whined softly while he put the plate down. Then at a command, the dog came out, cautiously took a bite of food---never taking its eyes off its master.

Lucien saw her, came to the car and stuck his head in through the open window. "What are you doing here?" he asked.

"I thought you might be wondering what happened to me this morning," Laurel spoke, her voice not betraying her nervousness. "I know I was wondering why you disappeared from the house."

"I saw that nosy Eva Farnsworth coming up the drive, so I left."

Laurel fought to keep her voice from breaking. "Do you even want to know what happened to my arms?"

"If you want me to know, you'll tell me." Lucien reached through the car window. His hand caressed her hair. "Would you like to come in?"

"No!" Laurel spat out the word.

"Fine," he replied as he quickly turned to walk away. He stopped, then spoke again. "I think it would be better if we didn't see each other any more."

"If that's what you want." Laurel replied. "But what about the Christmas party? Everyone will wonder why you're not there."

A smile played at the corner of Lucien's mouth. "Oh, I'll be there. You can count on it."

Laurel's tears did not come until she turned into the drive at Belle Rouge. She stopped the car in the front circle and leaned her head against the steering wheel. "What in the hell is wrong with me?" she asked. "Why am I crying over a man I hardly know. It's not as though I'm in love with him." She fumbled in her purse for a tissue and wiped her eyes. "Why am I trying to fool myself? I know what's wrong. It's been a long time since a man's been interested in going to bed with me. It felt good and I don't want to loose that feeling."

When the tears subsided, she wearily climbed out of the car and unlocked the front door. She threw her jacket on a chair beside the Christmas tree in the foyer and collapsed on the couch in the den. "I don't need Lucien Caulder," she said aloud.

She closed her eyes and her body relaxed. It seemed she had been dozing for only a moment when she awoke with a start. She was aware of some presence in the house. In the fading gray light of day she saw the outline of a person standing in the doorway. "Who's there?" she whispered, her voice unable to hide the fear. She rubbed the sleep from her eyes and stared into the hallway. "Is anyone there?"

When no answer came, she reached to turn on the table lamp. Cautiously, she crept into the foyer. The front door was standing open. Something drew her attention to the winding staircase. Then she heard it. It was the sound of boots shuffling on the steps, just beyond the turn of the stairs. Laurel caught her breath and started back toward the light in the den. But as she crossed the hallway a crunching sound beneath her feet froze her in her tracks. The light caught on the pieces of glass scattered on the floor. It was the antique Christmas ornaments she had found in the chest Barney sold her---the ones she and Eva had placed on the Christmas tree. They alone had been singled out and smashed to bits.

## CHAPTER 9

Laurel stood at the paddock by the barn, reached over the fence and gently stroked the neck of her red mare. The horse moved closer and nuzzled her cheek. When Laurel heard footsteps on the gravel behind her, she turned around and said, "I knew you'd come."

"I've been waiting and watching the paper for your ad," Barney grinned. "Knew you'd be wanting to get started on the barn before it got cold."

Suddenly, the mare snorted and jerked away. She did not stop running until she reached the other side of the field. "What in the world got into her?" Laurel frowned.

"That's typical of her breeding, ma'am. They get spooked easy."

"Barney, was it you at the sale barn who told Allen Williams that Flame's colt would be a good horse to buy?"

"I don't recall it, Miz MacKenzie, if I did. Now, what'd you have in mind to do at the barn?"

"I want three stalls redone before the mares are ready to foal."

Barney walked down the runway of the barn, sticking his head into first one and then another of the stalls. "Won't take no time to fix these up. Looks to me like what you need most is a new staircase into the hay loft. Mr. Williams will probably want to store some hay up there and we don't want you fallin' down some rickety old ladder. Now do we?"

Barney worked with amazing speed. By the time Laurel came to the barn on third day, he was putting fresh straw into the stalls.

“I can’t believe you’ve already finished the stalls,” she exclaimed.

“I finished the steps, too, last night after you went to the house. And Mr. Williams must have brought the hay early this morning before I got here. Come on up and see.”

The sweet aroma of the hay met them as Barney led the way into the loft. Laurel sat down on one of the bales. “You’ve done a wonderful job. I don’t know what I’d do without you.”

“I’m glad to be of service, ma’am. I hated to watch this place run down.”

“You once told me you lived in Cedarville all your life, Barney. What can you tell me about Belle Rouge?”

“Only a little bit, Miz MacKenzie. A few tales passed down, that’s all.”

“What kind of tales?” Laurel prodded. “Ghost stories?”

Barney stared into some distant space. “It’s hard for folks to rest when the truth ain’t fully known.”

“What truth, Barney? Tell me.”

“Ain’t my place, ma’am. I can only help you around the farm.”

Laurel was persistent. “That little book you found in the fireplace. It belonged to Lily Kilgore. She was the wife of the man who built Belle Rouge. They had a daughter, Claire. I have a feeling she kept a diary, too. Can you help me find it?”

“Don’t know, ma’am, but if I was a young’un I’d keep it in a secret place.”

“Claire loved horses. Was the barn her secret place?”

"Sounds reasonable, Miz MacKenzie. If I was her, I'd put it in a dark place nobody would notice. Say over there." Barney pointed toward the northeast corner of the loft.

Following the point of the old man's finger, Laurel made her way to where the slant of the roof seemed to meet the floor. She reached into the shadows and to her surprise found an invisible opening. Her fingers groped in the space until they touched something. Laurel pulled out a box. "It's a jewelry box," she exclaimed as she opened it. "It's empty," her voice fell.

Barney's gnarled hand examined the lining. "Sometimes folks hid things under here," he said. His fingers stopped at a slight bulge.

"Let me see," Laurel said as she carefully pulled back the lining. "It's a false bottom."

She turned the box over, shook it and out fell a book. "It's Claire's diary! I know it is! Look Barney, look at...." The old man had disappeared.

Jane and Eva left the courthouse and drove toward Belle Rouge. "I want to stop at one more place before we talk to Laurel," Eva said. The station wagon turned onto River Street and followed it till it came to a dead end.

"Why did you come to the old graveyard?" Jane asked.

"Just a hunch," Eva replied.

"Who do you think you're going to find?"

Eva stopped the car, got out, and followed by Jane, made her way to the edge of the burial ground. "When the Historical Society had this graveyard cleared, I found that Doctor James is buried here. The rest of his family moved back to my great-grandmother's home in Virginia when Doctor James died. They wanted to be close to relatives. In fact, they were visiting there when their house burned down. They'd lost everything. Why come back?"

"Everything?" Jane asked.

"Yes. Why?"

"How can you have Doctor James's record book if everything was lost?"

"That's a good question. It couldn't have been in the house when it burned," Eva replied. "He would have trusted Sheriff Miller with it. Is he buried here?"

"No. He's in our family graveyard at the old farm."

Eva stood beside her great-grandfather's stone for a moment then proceeded down the row. "You go down the back row, Jane. I know there's something here we need to find."

Jane had taken only a few steps when she called back to Eva. "I think I know what it is," she said. "I've just found Sumner Kilgore's grave."

The two women were headed out of town when Eva asked. "Do you know if there's a family graveyard at Belle Rouge?"

"I'm sure there is," Jane answered. "All farm owners had one in those days."

"Then why isn't the owner of Belle Rouge buried there?"

They were passing Hickory Ridge Training Center, when Jane said, "There's Lucien's car. I wish I knew how he fits into this puzzle."

A few minutes later, Eva turned into the drive at Belle Rouge. "I have a feeling we'll have to piece all the other parts together before we find that one."

A haggard Laurel MacKenzie met them at the front door. "Have you been writing all night?" Eva asked.

"No. I've been reading. I've found Claire's diary. I knew she had one."

"Where was it?"

"In the loft of the barn, Jane. Barney and I..."

"Barney's been here again?"

"Yes, Eva."

"What kind of feelings do you get when you're with this Barney?"

"Good ones. I like him. He said he was here to help me around the farm. Those were his exact words. He's here to help me."

"Maybe guide you would be the more correct term," Eva replied.

"I hope he's here to help solve the mystery of what's going on in this house," Laurel added.

"Has something else happened?"

"Yes. Do you remember the antique Christmas ornaments I found in the furniture I bought from Barney? You cut yourself on one when we were decorating. I found them smashed on the floor. None of the other bulbs---only those."

"There's some energy here that doesn't want us to solve the mystery," Eva frowned.

"But that only makes me want to know more," Laurel said.

"This is getting more dangerous as we find more information," Jane shuttered. "And I'm really getting frightened. What we found at the courthouse today confirms every person's name you mentioned Laurel. This is too coincidental. And we found Sumner Kilgore's grave in the community graveyard, but none of the rest of his family are there."

"Tell me everything you've found," Laurel demanded.

"First, do you know if there's a family graveyard on your farm?" Eva asked.

"Yes. It's beyond the race track. I found it while I was mowing this fall. I didn't bother to look at any of the gravestones."

"Could we go there?"

"Sure. We can drive there in my truck."

The graveyard was overgrown with honeysuckle and briars, making it difficult to walk. But they had little trouble spotting the main stone with the Kilgore name on it. Just in front of it was Lily's grave. To the right, Ross was buried. But Sumner Kilgore's space was empty. The search for Claire's grave site proved to be more difficult, because it was isolated and behind some evergreen shrubs.

"That's amazing," Jane said. "There's not a vine or a briar on it. It's as though someone is taking care of it."

"Where would the slaves be buried?" Laurel asked.

"Probably at the edge or just over the wall in their own section," Eva replied.

"Yes, there they are," Jane pointed.

Various names were carved into the stones along with what appeared to be the date of death. The three women moved among them until Laurel stopped.

"Here's Genevieve's grave."

"Look how it's sunk in," Jane shuddered. "It almost looks as if someone's tried to dig it up."

Laurel touched the stone. "What is it?" Eva asked.

"Nothing. It just feels warm."

Laurel headed back toward the truck. Jane started to follow, but when she became aware Eva was not with her, she went back.

"What are you looking at?" she asked.

"I can't find the black jockey's stone."

Eva and Jane were on their way back to Cedarville when Jane asked a question. "This Kilgore slave, Barnabas. Do you think Barney is related to him?"

"Maybe so."

"And why wouldn't Laurel let us read Claire's diary?"

"She said it was because she wanted to read it alone first," Eva replied.

Laurel had read the first half of Claire's diary the previous night. In it she read of the little girl's love for her brother and her love of horses. She also realized that at an early age Claire was aware of the discord in her father and mother's marriage. The diary told of how she tried to please her parents and ease her brother's pain.

As Laurel read on, Claire's writing began to display a refinement, a polish far beyond her years.

Laurel recalled her agent's critique of her own writing. "Your characters are not real", he had said. "Give them more emotion."

In the diary before her was a young girl's life written with the emotion Laurel knew she herself had failed to capture in her own writing.

She once again picked up the book and noticed a page that was blank except for the date. Laurel reached for Lily's diary and opened it to the last page. The dates were identical. It was the day of Lily and Ross' death.

She stared at the two books as they lay side by side. "That's strange," she said. "I thought maybe Claire had made the last entry in her mother's diary, but the handwriting is definitely not the same."

Laurel thumbed through several blank pages in Claire's book, then stopped at the next date entered. Claire had resumed her writing two years after the deaths.

*My father drinks constantly. The deaths of Mother and Ross still hang over him like a dark cloud. I can no longer reach him. When he's in his drunken stupors he calls me 'Lily'. I have lost my entire family.*

Laurel nestled down on the couch. Claire's voice seemed to invade the silence of Belle Rouge.

*March 5, 1882*

*I cannot believe that father agreed with Dr. James when he said I needed to get away from the farm for a little while. I am astonished that he consented to let me go to Louisville to visit with mother's friend, Alexandra Lennox. It seems so strange to me to call someone 'friend'. Father was always gone to New Orleans, Mother was always painting, and there was never an opportunity to cultivate friendships. Ross and I had only each other. These two years without Mother and Ross have been the loneliest time of my life.*

*I was afraid Mrs. Lennox would finally give up and stop inviting me. But I should have known better. It was through Mrs. Lennox's insistence that Mother, Ross and I ever got to attend any theatre openings in Louisville. I remember those trips as the most exciting times in my childhood. The moment we left Belle Rouge behind, my mother became one of those joyful people in her paintings. I now know it was my father's presence that imprisoned her creativness and her exciting personality.*

*How remarkable it was that Mrs. Lennox became our friend. On a trip to Europe, she saw Mother's parents perform for the last time at La Scala. She was so impressed with them she asked if she could purchase the portrait of my grandmother that hung in the lobby. She was informed that my mother, Lily, was the artist. When Mrs. Lennox asked how she might contact my mother, she was told that she had married Sumner Kilgore of Kentucky.*

*Of course the Lennox family knew of Sumner Kilgore. Mrs. Lennox, as Mother told me, came to visit shortly after I was born.*

*Mother was so happy to find someone who admired her parents that she donated several of her paintings to be hung in the MacCallum Theatre, which was named after Alexandra Lennox's family. I didn't realize, at my young age, what this friendship meant to my mother. How happy I am that Mrs. Lennox wants to continue this friendship with me. I'm sure this trip will be as exciting as all the others, even though it will bring back bittersweet memories of Mother and Ross.*

*I have decided to take my diary with me to record every day's happenings during this coming week, for Father may not allow such an excursion again.*

*March 23, 1882*

*My journey has finally begun. This lightness of spirit I feel has to be exactly what my mother felt when she left Belle Rouge and Sumner Kilgore behind.*

*My ever-faithful confidant and friend, Barnabas, drove me to the junction to catch the train. Father insisted Genevieve accompany me. I noticed Barnabas did not seem to mind that his wife would be gone.*

*Mrs. Lennox, even though she insists I call her Alexandra (I cannot bring myself to do it), has a glorious time planned for us. She says she is so happy to have a young person here with her to spoil, since her daughter is, as she puts it, "traipsing all over the world with her husband, who is an anthropologist (Mrs. Lennox's husband died many years ago). Tomorrow she will take me shopping for a gown to wear to the opening of a play at the MacCallum Theatre.*

*What a dear Barnabas is. He warned me about the young suitors who'd come round to meet Mrs. Lennox's beautiful young friend. My father warned me about the young men who would like nothing better than to court Sumner Kilgore's daughter to get their hands on Belle Rouge.*

*How my lonely existence needs to be filled with new people. Lately, I have dreamed several times of being in a crowded room. Across the room I see a young man whose back is to me. Slowly he turns around, but I wake before his face becomes clear. Will I find this mysterious person waiting for me before the end of this journey?*

*I thank God for Mrs. Lennox, and I will be eternally grateful to Dr. James for convincing my father to let me go to the city.*

*I will take just a moment to write a little more about this wonderful day. Mrs. Lennox came to pick me up at the railway station in an elegant carriage drawn by two magnificent black horses. My room at the hotel is just a few doors from the Lennox suite. For the first time in my life, I feel such freedom. If only Genevieve would stop hovering over me! But I suppose father has directed her to keep an eye on me. I made it very clear to her to stay in her room until I ring.*

*March 25, 1882*

*I have had no time to write these last two days. Alexandra and I have been to the dressmaker to be fitted for our gowns (they will be delivered tomorrow). We picnicked at a park by the river today after our trip to the art museum. I almost felt mother's presence with us. Tonight we will dine in the Crystal Room here at the hotel.*

*What a wonderful ending to a wonderful day. While we were waiting for our food to be served tonight, I went to the anteroom to look at Mother's paintings. A young man stood, totally engrossed, in front of one. I cannot believe I summoned enough courage to speak to him, but I did. "She would be so happy to know you appreciate her work," I said.*

*"Have you met the artist?" he asked.*

*"Lily was my mother," I proudly replied.*

*I cannot believe the blue of his eyes. I have not been able to get his eyes, or him, off my mind. I wonder who he is. I wonder if he lives in Louisville, for his accent is French. Will I ever see him again?*

*March 26, 1882*

*My gown was delivered this morning. It is a cream-colored silk, off the shoulders. Alexandra says it is the same color as my hair. The long gloves set the dress off beautifully. I have to rush because Alexandra has made an appointment for me to get my hair styled. She said it is time I look the part of mistress of Belle Rouge.*

*I wonder if HE'LL be there tonight. I could not bring myself to ask Alexandra if she knows him.*

*What a glorious surprise. Not only was he at the play, but he was the lead actor. I feel he is the character portrayed in the play, for you could tell the words and emotions came from his soul.*

*Alexandra knows him well. She brought him here from Paris. I could hardly contain myself when we were introduced. I don't even know what I said. Philippe Dumont. How beautiful it sounds.*

*March 27, 1882*

*I cannot believe the generosity Alexandra has shown me. She has ordered an entire wardrobe to replace my outdated clothing. One casual outfit has just arrived, for we-Alexandra, Philippe and I-will take an excursion today on the river. I know she can see just how much I am attracted to him. If only he could feel the same. But I dare not hope, because I could not face his rejection.*

*I panicked tonight. I thought I had misplaced my diary. God forbid that anyone would read my private thoughts. Genevieve found it on the nightstand. I'm surprised I left it there. I always keep it in my jewelry box. I suppose, in my excitement, I left it out.*

*I felt my heart would burst when Philippe brought us back to the hotel, for he kissed my hand. Could he possibly care for me?*

*March 28, 1882*

*I have little time to write. Philippe is taking me to a rehearsal at the theatre. Alexandra isn't feeling well. She said the cast of the play could be my chaperone for today.*

*Even the rain could not dampen my spirits. Philippe had the hotel send us a picnic lunch, and after the rehearsal, we ate backstage. How thoughtful and considerate he is. I feel as if I've known him for years. He is as easy to talk to as Barnabas.*

*April 1, 1882*

*I am in love with Philippe Dumont. I have not written in this diary for several days because there is no way to express my feelings. I cannot find the words.*

*Today, Alexandra gave me a letter my mother wrote just weeks before she died. Her request was that Alexandra give me the letter when she believed I had found the man I could love. I cherish her words and will keep them forever.*

*One question, though, keeps gnawing at me. Did my mother know she was going to die?*

*April 3, 1882*

*How I have dreaded the end of my visit. Tomorrow I must leave for home. I have not been able to bear the thought that I may never see Philippe again. But fate has taken care of the situation.*

*Genevieve left two days ago under mysterious conditions, and now I know why. Father has wired to say he called her home to prepare for the celebration of my eighteenth birthday. He requested that Alexandra and any new friends be invited to accompany me to Belle Rouge to join in the festivities.*

*April 4, 1882*

*Barnabas was all smiles when he picked us up at the station today. He looked grand in his new black suit. Father waited at Belle Rouge to greet us. I found him cool and reserved. Perhaps it is because this is the first time he has hosted a party in a very long time. I cannot tell if he likes Philippe, but he is cordial to him.*

*Barnabas must like him. He scurries around, making sure our guest's needs are met. Who could tell anything about Genevieve! She is efficient, though.*

*April 5, 1882*

*Philippe and I rode over the farm today. He seems to be quite impressed with Belle Rouge.*

*How coincidental life can be. He told me his father had a racing stable in France. That is the first time he has mentioned anything about himself. I would like to know more, but I don't feel I should pry. Philippe kissed me. Oh, how I love him and want to be his wife.*

*April 6, 1882*

*One could not ask for a more beautiful day for a party. Alexandra had a red dress made for me just for this occasion. Her gifts are so wonderful. After dinner, she asked me to accompany her to her room, where she gave me a ruby necklace. She said she loves me like a daughter. How I love her!*

*My father has surprised me to no end by the way he has attended to the details of my party. Though Alexandra denies it, she must have advised him. He has had white lilies brought in. Hundreds and hundreds of white lilies adorn our home. I will write more later. Genevieve is here to help me dress. Even she has a smile on her face. At least I think it's a smile.*

*PHILIPPE LOVES ME! We found time to slip away from the party, and he asked me if he had my permission to speak to my father. Oh yes, oh yes! He will do it tomorrow.*

*Alexandra seemed surprised when I told her we planned to marry. Surely she could see how much Philippe and I love one another.*

*A soft knock came at my door about midnight tonight. I knew who it was instantly. Perhaps it is not right, but I let him in. I so love him. I will marry him. It can't be wrong. Nothing can be wrong that can make a person feel loved.*

*Though he has gone now, I can still feel the warmth of his body against mine. The sweetness of him lingers on my pillow. I am now truly his.*

*April 7, 1882*

*I accompanied Alexandra to the train. I know she asked me to come to Louisville again in the fall, but I could hardly concentrate on what she was saying, for Philippe will talk to Father while we are gone. When I write next in this diary, we will have begun our wedding plans.*

Laurel became acutely aware of her body's stiffness and the waning light. Somewhere in the distance, she heard the neighing of a horse. "I know I'm late with the feed. Just hold on till I find a flashlight."

She made her way to the kitchen, ran her hand against the wall and finally found the light switch. She retrieved the flashlight from the cabinet drawer and hurried out of the house. She shuddered in the brisk night air, wishing she had remembered her jacket.

"That's strange," she thought, "all three mares are usually waiting for me at the barn door." She mixed the grain in the buckets and carried them to the feedlot. When the mares did not respond to her whistle, she stood quietly and listened.

Two distinct whinnies came from the direction of the graveyard. "Well, come on!" she yelled impatiently. Then she heard it--one high-pitched cry of pain. "Oh god, no. That's Flame." She ran back to the house, found her keys and jumped into the truck.

The headlights picked up Allen Williams' mares standing beside the stone wall of the graveyard. Her mare was no where to be seen. Laurel braked to a stop and ran to the wall. Flame was lying on her side, tangled in the honeysuckle and unable to get up.

Laurel crawled over the fence and the mare tried to lift her head. "Come on girl. Get up. You can do it." She tugged on the halter, but the mare heaved a sigh and made no other attempt to move.

Laurel heard the crack of a twig behind her. She wheeled around and the beam from the flashlight came to rest on Barney's face.

“Ain’t no use, ma’am”, the old man shook his head. “Her back’s broke. I’m so sorry,” he said. “I’m sorry I didn’t get here in time.”

## CHAPTER 10

Laurel cautiously opened the front door of her home in response to the knock. She could only stare at the young woman standing in front of her.

"Aren't you going to invite me in?"

"Of course, Beth. Come in. I wasn't expecting you till tomorrow. I guess I was a little taken back."

"Taken back? By what, Mother?"

"You look more---more grown up."

"More grown up than you've ever bothered to notice would probably be the correct way to put it."

Laurel snatched up her daughter's suitcase. "Maybe I should amend my statement. You're more grown up---in some respects. But you still make your childish remarks."

The anger was apparent in Beth's eyes for only a second. Then she smiled. "You're the same as always, Mother."

Laurel sighed. "Why do we do this to each other? Could we please start over with this conversation? I'm glad to see you. I'm happy you came."

Beth squelched her inclination to make another remark. Instead she simply replied, "Me too."

"Come into the kitchen. Maybe you'd like something hot to drink."

The aroma of cinnamon filled the kitchen as Laurel poured the tea.

Beth lifted the cup to her lips. "The house looks like you."

"Glad you like it."

"I didn't say that. It's not my style. It simply matches you."

"You mean 'old'?" Laurel quipped. "I'm sorry," she checked herself. "I'm not going to have a game of words with you. We've done enough of that in our lifetime."

"Why stop now, Mother? Besides, you always win the game." Beth took a lump of sugar and watched it dissolve in the brown liquid. "You know---it was only recently I realized how you manage to get the last word. You make me lose my temper. When I do that I can't think of anything else to say. Then you win the game. But I've decided it's not going to happen this time. I will not let you make me angry."

"Good," Laurel managed a smile. "We don't need to spend Christmas antagonizing one another. Why didn't you let me know the exact time you were coming? I could have picked you up at the airport."

"I wanted to take a taxi."

"Why in the world would you spend the money to do that when I could have....I'm sorry, again, Beth. It's your money."

"No, actually it isn't. It's Dad's. By giving me money he found a way to get rid of some of the guilt he had by not inviting me home for Christmas. Actually, he said I could come home, but I'd have to sleep on the couch. His new wife's two daughters are occupying my room."

"Beth, I'm sorry."

"Good grief, Mother! How many times are you going to say you're sorry? It's not necessary."

"But I know how much you love your father. It must be difficult."

Beth took a sip of tea. "Your sympathy is quite unnerving, quite different. I've never thought of you as having sympathy for anyone except yourself."

Laurel jumped to her feet. "I said there will be none of this while you're here. Do you understand me? If you can't abide by what I say, then you may leave."

Beth made no attempt to reply. She simply watched as her mother stomped out of the room. Then she poured herself another cup of tea.

Karen Williams stopped walking her horse when she saw the Ranger pull into the driveway at Hickory Ridge. "Allen, Laurel's here," she called.

The vet was just coming out of her colt's stall when Laurel entered the barn. "What's happened?" she asked.

"Red Satan has a lung infection," Allen replied. "His temperature's 105 degrees. If the heat goes to his feet, we're in trouble."

"What can we do?" Laurel asked.

"Antibiotics and a hosing down of his legs to keep them cool. That's about it."

The alarm was apparent in Laurel's voice. "Allen, you know what happened to my mare. I can't lose Satan, too."

"He'll have to be turned out for a while after we get him well," the vet interjected.

"How long?" Laurel asked.

"Several weeks. He may come 'round in a hurry after the rest. You just never know."

Laurel could not bring herself to return home immediately. Instead, she turned the Ranger toward Cedarville. The knowledge of Red Satan's illness had only served to remind her of the sight of her mare dying in agony while she and Barney stood by, unable to comfort her.

She drove through town and made a left. "Maybe it wasn't meant for me to have horses," she thought. "Maybe I was a fool to even move here."

In a few minutes, Laurel pulled to a stop in Eva's driveway. "Come in," Eva greeted her. "I'm in the parlor. I was just reading Doctor James' record book again."

"Have you uncovered anything new?"

"I don't think so. But I have come to the conclusion Doctor James may have known his life was in danger. From what Jane and I pieced together, he must have given his book to someone, or it would have burned with the house."

"How did you get the book, Eva?"

"My mother gave it to me. Jane and I believe Preston Miller had it for safekeeping. We believe he gave it to my grandfather, who was Doctor James's youngest son, when he came back here to settle with his family. Have you read any more of Claire's diary?"

"I haven't had a chance, not with the mare's accident, Beth coming a little early, and now Red Satan's fever."

"I think your colt will be fine."

"I hope that's your psychic ability coming through."

"Your horse will be racing by May," Eva said confidently.

"Tell me about your daughter."

"I'd hoped you could meet her before the Christmas party, but I think Beth needs to catch up on her sleep. She's been sleeping till noon these past few days."

"I'm looking forward to meeting her."

"She'll like you, Eva. She needs someone to talk to. I know all these changes in her life are really bothering her. I think she'll probably open up and talk to you. God knows I can't talk to her without a fight. I don't understand why she acts the way she does toward me."

"Give her a little more time."

"She's old enough to graduate from college this spring. How much more time will it take?" Laurel glanced at her watch. "I guess I'd better go. Beth will be hungry when she gets up."

Eva went back to the parlor after Laurel left. She picked up Doctor James's record book once more, but she could not concentrate on it. Thoughts of Laurel and her daughter would not leave her mind.

She could not help but wonder if they had competed for the attention of the man who was so prominent in both their lives. She wondered if Laurel believed Beth had won the affection of Robert Bradford away from her.

Lucien Caulder was washing his horse after its workout, when he saw Laurel's truck pass Hickory Ridge going in the direction of Belle Rouge.

The vet was getting in his vehicle when Lucien stopped him. "How's Miss MacKenzie's two-year-old?" he asked.

"Touch and go for a while, but he'll be okay. We caught the infection just in time. Lucky that Karen came back to the Center during the night, or he might be dead."

"Lucky indeed," Lucien replied and he jerked on his horse's lead shank and headed back into the barn.

Beth was not yet up when Laurel returned home, so Laurel retrieved Lily's and Claire's diaries from the den and headed for the glass room. She had just sat down to read when she heard Beth calling her. For some reason she hid the books inside a loose board in the floor of the room. Then she went back downstairs.

Beth stood in the middle of the foyer toweling off her long, straight black hair. "Where's your dryer, Mom? I forgot mine."

"In the bathroom cabinet. Please put it back when you're finished. What do you want for lunch?"

Beth headed for the bathroom. "I don't care. Whatever's handy."

"You've lost weight," Laurel called after her. "You need to eat."

"Good God, Mom! Can't you hear? I don't care what you fix. I'll eat it."

Beth put on a black jogging suit trimmed in white. She applied a stark white foundation and vivid red lipstick and accentuated her dark eyes with eyeliner and mascara. As she entered the kitchen, she couldn't help but notice her mother's look of disapproval.

"Are you going somewhere?" Laurel asked.

"For a jog, that's all."

"Why so dressed up?"

"I don't like the natural look you prefer, Mom. It reeks of letting oneself go. Don't you think?"

Laurel consciously stuffed down a response. "I thought you might like to help me finish decorating for a dinner party I'm having on Saturday."

"A dinner party in Cedarville? Who in the world in this god-forsaken place would come to 'dinner'?"

"It's the county historical society. If you'd give these people a chance, you might like them."

"Can't you find anything duller to occupy your time?"

"That's enough, Beth. Go for your run. Maybe it'll sweeten your humor."

"Don't set a place for me at your dinner party, Mom. If you'll lend me your car, I'll find something else a little more fun to do that night, maybe in Louisville."

"Like hell you will," Laurel muttered to herself. "Not unless you want to jog the twenty five miles."

At Laurel's request, Eva and Jane came a few hours early on Saturday. She was just putting the finishing touches on the dining room table when they arrived.

"The house is absolutely beautiful," Jane exclaimed.

"And just look at the table," Eva added. "Everything's white, white and gold."

Laurel lifted the lace tablecloth. "This is the table I bought from Barney. Look at the grain. It's mahogany. And just think, the Kilgores actually sat here when they had dinner."

"Somehow, that's not too appealing to me," Eva shuttered.

"I wish I had the rest of chairs that go with it," Laurel sighed.

"Did you ask Barney if he knew where they were?"

"Yes I did, Jane. He said he only had these two."

"Maybe they'll show up."

"The place where you'll find them may be another part of this puzzle," Eva said. She glanced into the kitchen. "Where's your daughter?"

"Certainly not in there. It's a little beneath her to help out. She's in her room pouting. She wanted to go into Louisville to find a more lively crowd. I refused to give her the car keys."

"Surely she wouldn't go alone to a unfamiliar town," Jane frowned.

"You don't know Beth."

"Her mother goes places alone. She even moved to a strange city by herself," Eva quipped.

The annoyance was apparent in Laurel's voice. "This situation is a little different."

Eva glanced over Laurel's shoulder. "You must be Beth," she smiled at the young woman entering the room. "My, what a pretty red dress."

"Do you like it too, Mother?"

"If you were going to some bar, it might be appropriate."

"But I'm not. I'm here tonight to meet all your new Cedarville friends."

The turnout for the dinner party at Belle Rouge was larger than most get-togethers for the Historical Society, Jane assured Laurel. But it was not the number of people in attendance that made Laurel a bit nervous, it was the absence of one.

Just as the last person found a seat, a knock was heard at the door.

"I'll get it, Mother," Beth said.

It was a few moments before Beth reappeared, clinging to the arm of Lucien Caulder.

## CHAPTER 11

Laurel saw very little of Beth in the days before Christmas. Her daughter spent most of her time with Eva. Though she felt a tinge of jealously because Beth did not relish her company, she gladly spent her time reading Claire's diary.

The weather was unusually warm on this particular mid-December day, and a misty rain had fallen continuously for over twenty-four hours when Laurel made her way to the glass room.

She lifted the loose floorboard, extracted Claire's diary and settled in to her reading.

*Philippe and I have not had the privacy to discuss his talk with my father. He whispered to me at supper that he would once again be at my door tonight. I hear him now.*

Laurel jumped at the sound of pounding on a door. It came from somewhere on the second floor. Slowly, she crept down the ladder. The figure of Sumner Kilgore manifested itself.

"Claire! You hear me?" Kilgore's voice roared. "Open this door before I break it down!"

Panic gripped Claire. "Philippe! Oh, Philippe, my father will kill you if he finds you in my bedroom. Get dressed quickly. You can climb out the window."

"I refuse to run from him. He knows I want to marry you. He can't refuse when he sees we've been together. Open the door. There's nothing to fear."

At the click of the lock, Sumner Kilgore burst through the door and lunged at Philippe Dumont.

"No, Daddy! Leave him alone. I beg you. We're going to be married!"

"Do you think I'd let you marry a man like this?" Sumner growled. "He's already married one young girl and taken her for every cent she had. Can't you see he's trying the same thing again?"

"That's not true!" Claire cried. "How can you know anything about him? You just met him."

"I have ways to find things out. My facts are straight. You can rest assured on that."

Claire turned to her lover. "Philippe, tell him he has the wrong person."

"Yes, maybe it would be better if the words came from your mouth, Dumont. Do you have a wife elsewhere? Tell her, you bastard. Tell her the truth, or I'll kill you here on the spot."

"It's...it's all true," Philippe stammered.

Claire stared at him in disbelief. "No, it can't be. You asked me to marry you."

Kilgore seemed to relax. "Of course he did. He's out of money."

"Philippe, how could you? You said you loved me."

"Oh, that's not all there is to Mr. Dumont's story. Genevieve," Sumner called. Bring in that wretched creature. I was saving this for tomorrow, daughter, but I think now is a perfect time."

A frail young woman timidly entered the room as Kilgore continued. "Do you see this woman, Claire? Do you see that pitiful child in her arms? If you had continued with Philippe Dumont, this is what you would look like a year from now.

Scream all you want, daughter, but I have saved you from this horrible fate. Go ahead, Claire. Scream!"

That morning, Jane had wakened with a start, the details of a dream still vivid on her mind. She took a notebook and a pencil from the drawer of the nightstand and began to write.

"You certainly had my desk clerk up in arms, Preston," Alexandra Lennox laughed. "I can just see him at your hotel."

Miller, somewhat self-conscious, followed her down the hallway. He had never felt comfortable in her presence. She was unlike any woman he had ever known---self-assured in her business ventures and, he would guess, in her intimate relationships.

He had never allowed himself to think of her as anyone other than a friend. He convinced himself he was indeed fortunate to call her that.

"Oh, you don't know how good it feels to laugh," Alexandra sighed. "There's not been much to laugh about lately."

"No, ma'am," Preston Miller responded. "Not if you're referring to the Kilgores."

"How is Claire?"

"Timothy's worried about her." Miller said as he studied Mrs. Lennox's face. He could see it in her eyes just as she recognized it in his: They shared Dr. James' and Lily's secret.

"Of course," Alexandra thought, "Preston Miller would be Dr. James' confidant, just as she had been Lily's. But now was not the time to discuss it. There was more pressing business at hand."

Alexandra opened the door of the Lennox suite. "I take the liberty of using your first name, Preston. Why have you not used mine?"

"I wouldn't do that with any lady, unless I was invited."

"Consider this a formal invitation," she returned his smile.

When they entered the sitting room, a handsome young man in his thirties, dressed in English riding boots and a tweed jacket, rose from his chair.

"Preston, I'd like you to meet my nephew, Bruce MacCallum. Bruce, this is my good friend, Preston Miller. Sit down, both of you. I want to discuss some business. But first, Bruce, would you get the Scotch?"

"Do I smell a scheme, Alexandra?" Miller asked.

"Perhaps you simply have a nose for the fragrance of excellent Scotch," she teased.

Bruce MacCallum poured three glasses. "Has my aunt told you anything about her plan?" he asked.

"No, but I knew something had to be up when I got a wire asking me to come here. I have a feeling it has something to do with the Kilgores."

"Oh yes, indeed it does," Alexandra replied. "You bought a horse named Shadow Dancer from Sumner. Claire raised him and trained him, and Sumner sold him to you without consulting her. Is that correct?"

Preston Miller set his glass on the table. "Mrs. Lennox, I did not come here for a scolding. I was unaware that Claire didn't want to sell when I bought the colt. The horse simply looked good to me, and Sumner wanted to get rid of it."

"Preston, wait! I'm sorry. I didn't mean to give you the impression I was scolding. I simply wanted to state the facts. I can sometimes be a little brusque. Let me start over and tell you what I have in mind."

Miller sat back down and took another drink as Alexandra began.

"Bruce and his brother train my horses in Europe. We haven't raced here in the states yet. But I think it's time we did. I don't intend to bring my stock over. I'm going to buy here."

"And you want Shadow Dancer?" Miller questioned.

"I hear he's an excellent prospect to win the Gold Cup."

"I get the distinct impression you've never laid eyes on him, Alexandra. And you want to buy him?"

"Claire thinks a lot of him."

"And so do I. But I don't think it's your normal policy to choose a horse because a young girl likes it."

"Claire's not just any girl. She knows her horses. Besides, she told me you promised her you'd give Dancer a chance to prove himself. Have you begun his training?"

"I've hired no professional trainer. I've been doing it. I'm afraid I'll disappoint her. I can't get him ready in time."

Alexandra took a sip from her glass. "But you don't have to disappoint her. Here's my proposition. I'll pay Bruce to train Shadow Dancer for half interest. You'll own half, I'll own half. It will cost you nothing."

"I don't make snap decisions," Miller hesitated.

Alexandra re-filled his glass. "We don't have time to wait, Preston. Claire needs this. Have you seen her lately? I don't want her to end up like her mother. Can't you see that's what's going to happen if we don't do something?"

"My God! You can't believe she'll do what Lily did."

"It's possible. And I'll never forgive myself for my part in the Philippe Dumont fiasco. Don't you understand? I must do something. Seeing your horse win might pull her out of her depression."

"We don't have a jockey," Miller hesitated. "All the good ones are already signed on with the other entries."

"Can we get Barnabas away from Sumner?" Alexandra asked.

"No way. When Sumner killed Satan, he gave up a sure winner in the cup race. Only Barnabas' skill can give Sumner's other horse a winning chance. Besides, Barnabas is loyal to him."

"Why don't we get someone Barnabas has trained?"

"He hasn't trained anyone," Miller assured her.

"There's one. Claire."

"What?" Preston Miller rose to his feet. "Women can't ride in a race."

"Have you seen Claire ride?" Alexandra asked.

"Yes, she's very good. She could ride Satan as well as Barnabas could. But, for God's sake, she's a female."

"She needn't look like one when she rides, Preston. Our trainer's from Europe. It stands to reason the jockey would be too. French. Yes, that's it. That's why he doesn't talk to anyone. That's why he's shy and doesn't mingle. He'll disappear, go back to Europe right after the race."

Miller leaned his head back against the chair and closed his eyes. "I'm about to make a pact with the devil himself," he sighed.

"Herself," Alexandra winked and filled his glass once more.

Eva glanced at the clock. Her visitor was more than two hours late. When she heard the car in the driveway, she opened the door. "Come in, Beth. I was a little worried."

Beth brushed past her. "I thought I'd take a drive."

Eva took Beth's jacket and placed it over the back of a kitchen chair. "There's been so much rain. I was afraid you'd had an accident."

"You remind me of my grandmother, Mrs. Farnsworth. She used to worry over me."

"Laurel's mother?"

"Gosh no. She was worse than Mom. Never had any time for anyone."

Eva led Beth into the parlor. "Is that the way your mother seems to you?"

"She's busy writing," Beth sighed. "It consumes her."

"Yes," Eva agreed. "It does indeed."

Laurel sat in the glass room. She could see Dr. James' buggy pull to a stop in front of the house. Claire was waiting for him.

"Well young lady, don't you look fine today," he greeted her.

"I'm feeling better. I was on my way to the stables. Barnabas is going to work Scarlet Satan."

"The horse Sumner's running in the Gold Cup?" Doctor James inquired.

"Yes. Barnabas says she's coming around quite well. Of course she's not Red Satan, but she's good. Barnabas says she can win. There are only two other entries we know of that might upset her: the bay mare from Tennessee and the Virginia stallion."

Doctor James laughed. "I know Claire Kilgore's feeling better when she starts all this horse talk."

"I didn't mean to bore you," she apologized.

"You could never do that, Claire." The doctor put his arm around her shoulders, but when he felt her tense, he quickly took his arm away.

"Doctor James, did you know Sheriff Miller's going to enter Dancer in the Cup?"

"I don't think so. He told me he doesn't have a trainer."

"But he promised me he would," she protested. "That was the only good thing about selling my horse. Dancer would have a chance to show how good he is."

Dr. James could see Claire's disappointment, and he added, "I could be mistaken."

"If Dancer hasn't been trained specifically for the Gold Cup, it wouldn't be right to enter him," Claire sighed. "He couldn't win."

Claire slowed her steps and stopped. "I'm not feeling well. If you'll excuse me, I'll go back to my room."

Doctor James followed her as she took a short cut through the kitchen. Genevieve paused to observe them.

"See, Miss Claire," she said. "I told you you were too weak to go outside. You best stay in your bed. I'll bring you your drink as soon as I can fix it."

"What drink?" Doctor James asked curtly.

"Just my special tea, sir," Genevieve replied.

"I told you not to give her anything but regular food and drink. And if I ever hear of you doing that again, I'll go to Sumner."

"Mr. Sumner don't like you no more. He wouldn't believe anything you told him."

"You're wrong. He may not like me, but he knows I have Claire's best interest at heart. He'd believe me. He loves her, even if he doesn't show it."

"He loves..." Genevieve stopped. "The question is, Doctor James, who's he more likely to believe, me or you? If Mr. Sumner discovers your secret, he won't believe anything you say."

"You want a showdown, Genevieve? Remember this: Barnabas knows a lot, too. Who do you think he'd side with?

There's something else you should know. I've kept a record of everything you've done, and everything I suspect you've done. What if I show it to Sumner? What would he think of you then?"

Genevieve's eyes narrowed, and her fingernails dug into the palm of her hand as she watched the doctor climb the stairs. She despised him. He'd sparked a tiny bit of fear inside her. But she reassured herself, no one would stand in her way. She'd come too far.

"Don't you worry about which side Barnabas would come down on," she mumbled. "I don't know any man who can't be controlled when a good woman gets him in bed."

Barnabas adjusted the stirrups and swung himself onto Scarlet Satan's back. Wide-eyed, the chestnut filly tried to bolt, but Barnabas gathered a tight rein and the horse settled into a leisurely gallop.

When the warm-up was over, Barnabas pulled the horse up at an imaginary starting line on the back stretch. With a yell and a crack of the whip, he loosened the reins and the chestnut shot down the straightaway. The filly covered the half-mile track with blazing speed, and held the pace until they entered the stretch the second time. Barnabas struck the filly twice on the flank, but she was spent.

When horse and rider crossed the finish line, Barnabas hopped off and led the lathered animal back to the shed row. He'd almost finished wiping her down when Sumner Kilgore approached.

"What's the verdict?" Sumner asked.

Barnabas fastened a lead shank to the halter and turned the horse over to the hot-walker. "There's nothing I know of can run with Scarlet Satan for a mile, maybe a mile and a quarter. Mile and a half---I don't know. Tennessee mare's a good come from behind horse. She could catch her."

Sumner shook his head. "Scarlet Satan's the best I have now. She's trained well. She couldn't even run a mile when we started."

"It might have been a good idea to keep Miss Claire's Dancer colt. He had a lot of stamina," Barnabas added.

"Hell! I don't want to hear any more about that white-legged bastard. He couldn't have stood up to any kind of training. He would've been lame in no time. Scarlet's the best of the lot. Shadow Dancer will end up doing what he's best suited for...hauling Preston Miller's big ass around in a buggy."

Doctor James laid his hand on Claire's brow. "Good. No fever," he said.

"Why am I so tired all the time?" she asked.

"You've been through a lot in the last two years. Sometimes a body just needs to rest. But I think you're now ready for some activity," the doctor smiled.

"I don't know what I could do."

"Why not work with one of the yearlings?"

"My father would only sell it," she replied. "It's not easy to part with a horse if you become attached to it."

"It's never easy to part with a loved one, Claire."

"Things happen for the best, Doctor James. Unpleasant things need to be put out of your mind."

"Perhaps, my dear, that philosophy's all right after you've gone through all the stages of grief."

"Grieving only brings pain. I see no need for it."

Doctor James picked up his black bag. "If you find out how to avoid pain in life, let me know. Oh, I almost forgot. The station master gave me this wire for you. Alexandra Lennox is coming for a visit. She should brighten up this place."

When Beth had gone, Eva picked up Dr. James' record book. "Please, God. Let me find something this time."

Absentmindedly, she ran her finger down the inside of the book's spine. The pain of a paper cut made her wince. She bent the book farther back and saw that a page had been carefully cut out. She studied the pages on either side. Each one contained a family name and their health records.

"Jarvis," she read the name on the page before the missing one. "Lansing," she read on the following one. "Kilgore!" she said the name aloud. "That's what's missing---the page on the Kilgore family. Dr. James wrote other notes about the Kilgores in his book in several places. Why wouldn't he keep all their information in order?"

"A safety precaution?" she wondered. "Anyone thumbing through the book would assume all the Kilgore information would be on one page, just as the other families were. Anyone trying to destroy the Kilgore information might not realize these other pages were here if they weren't in alphabetical order."

Eva lit the white candle on the end table and sat back in her chair. "Help me," she prayed. "Please, Dr. James, help me."

Her mind flashed to a long forgotten picture in the family album, a photograph of Dr. James' house. She saw herself walking into the house and into her great-grandfather's office. Dr. James was seated at his desk, writing in the record book.

*I am now forced to watch as Lily's daughter follows in her mother's footsteps. Since the terrible episode with the Frenchman, Dumont, Claire too suffers from an illness similar to her mother's.*

*All medication has been taken from the house, but I have caught Gen giving her what she calls "special tea." I believe Gen wants to remove all women from the life of Sumner Kilgore. I know this is an extreme statement, but I believe it more and more each day. Gen is doing something to Claire. I know it. I will go to Sumner when I have enough proof.*

Eva saw Dr. James spring bolt upright in his chair. "Oh dear God, can it be that?" he exclaimed.

He went to the bookcase, ran his finger down the rows until he found the book he was looking for---*Voodoo in the African Culture.*

## CHAPTER 12

Beth's departure from Belle Rouge was as sudden as her arrival. On Christmas Eve, she announced she'd reconsidered her father's invitation. Over Laurel's objection, she left early Christmas morning, refusing to let her mother drive her to the airport.

Laurel and Jane celebrated the day at Eva's. They spent most of the time comparing what they'd uncovered about Belle Rouge and the Kilgore family.

Jane shared her dreams---the plan Alexandra Lennox presented to Preston Miller to enter Shadow Dancer in the Gold Cup Race, with Claire riding, and the most puzzling fact---Lily Kilgore and Doctor James had each confided some mysterious secret to Alexandra and Preston.

Eva said that after she'd discovered a page had been cut from Doctor James' record book, she'd envisioned him in his study as he came to the conclusion Genevieve was using some form of voodoo to destroy the Kilgore women who stood in her way of becoming mistress of Belle Rouge.

Laurel retold the diary's account of how cruel Sumner Kilgore was in his revelation of Philippe Dumont's real purpose in his courtship of Claire.

When they had each finished, it was Laurel who expressed her doubt, not in the diary's authenticity---that was a tangible thing---but in the credibility of dreams and visions. Were they not simply supposition or imagination?

Eva remained firm in her belief that the mind could see into the past. Jane was a little less ready to accept the validity of her dreams without some statistics to back them up.

Her cousin, John Miller, possessed some of Preston Miller's personal papers. Perhaps they might give a clue to the date of Preston's business trips and the names of those with whom he dealt. Maybe Alexandra's name would appear in them.

Jane was able to recall the name of a man who was doing research on the race tracks in the Louisville area. He could know something about the Cedarville track. The three women agreed to meet in one week to share their findings.

It was only a few days into that week when a deep depression descended on Laurel. The loneliness was overwhelming. She began to wonder if she'd acted too hastily in breaking off with Lucien. Wasn't having someone, anyone, around, better than this? Maybe if she talked to him.

Laurel had just turned onto the road to Caulder's house when she saw his car coming toward her. There was nowhere to go. She'd have to pass him.

Her fear of him seeing her was unnecessary, for he could hardly notice her when his attention was turned toward the dark haired woman nestled close to him.

Laurel waited until Lucien's car stopped at the intersection with the main road. She whipped the Ranger into a driveway, backed out and headed after them. Just as she stopped behind the car, it turned left toward Cedarville. Instead of following them, Laurel headed for Belle Rouge. She'd seen all she needed to see.

Her hand shook as she dialed the phone. Robert Bradford would surely be at work by this time. "Robert," she responded to his hello. "Is Beth there with you?"

Laurel knew what his answer would be. "No. She's all right. ---- We didn't exactly have a fight. ---- She's with a-a friend. ---- I'm sure. I saw her. ---- I've got to go. ---- I'll phone you later. Bye."

Laurel climbed the stairs to the glass room and retrieved Claire's diary from its hiding place.

*My brain is muddled. I don't want to be with anyone. I cannot bear to see my father. Doctor James visits, but if my father's here, he turns him away. I don't understand the anger between them, but I don't have the energy to question why. I vaguely remember seeing Barnabas at my door, but Genevieve sends him away. It is she alone who attends me. I now accept willingly her cup of bitter tea. It's the balm that soothes the hurt, so I drink.*

*The song Genevieve sings continuously is hypnotic. It must be a tune from somewhere in her past in the mysterious back country she comes from---so near to my mother's home.*

*I think of my mother often. I recall the day I last saw her, standing at the third floor windows. I remember how the sun caught on the shattered glass, surrounding her like a snow shower on a bright wintry day. Her white gown flowed as if she had wings. An angel fell, no longer able, no longer willing to fly.*

Laurel closed the diary and returned it to its hiding place. Through the frost-covered glass she could hear the icy snow flakes as they tapped gently on the panes. She closed her eyes. She saw Genevieve in the kitchen. The mulatto woman reached into her pocket, then sprinkled the powdery substance in her hand into the boiling water on the stove. She picked up a pillow that was lying on the table, placed something made of feathers inside and sewed the seam together.

Laurel was trembling when she came to herself. The cold had permeated her body, making it difficult to stand. She headed for her bedroom, turning on the hot water in the tub on her way.

She dialed Eva. "I need to talk. Will you ask Jane to meet us at your house?" Laurel paused for a second. "I know you're right about the visions and the dreams. I'll be there within the hour."

After a two-hour wait, Eva could no longer resist. "We're going to Laurel's," she announced to Jane. "Something's dreadfully wrong."

The back door of Belle Rouge was unlocked. There was a deathly silence as the two women entered. Then they heard it. Somewhere in the house, water was running.

Jane led the way as they sloshed down the hall toward Laurel's bedroom. "You don't think she'd do anything to...."

"Oh, God, look," Eva interrupted. She waded into the bathroom and shut off the water. "It must have been running since she called."

"Come quickly," Jane called from the bedroom.

Laurel cowered in the corner, her eyes in a frozen stare. In front of her on the floor lay a small, grotesque figure of a bird.

It was well into the evening when Laurel awoke in a strange room. When her eyes focused, she saw Eva and Jane seated on either side of the bed.

"We brought you to my house a few hours ago," Eva said. "How are you feeling?"

"I'm all right. Why am I here? Why am-----? Oh---" she sunk down into the covers. "I was getting ready to come to your house when-----"

"You don't have to talk," Jane assured her.

"I need to. I spent some time in the glass room this morning, reading Claire's diary. At least I think I was reading. It was almost as if I were speaking, feeling what Claire was going through. Eva, I know you're right about the mind's ability to go back into the past. I remember closing my eyes and---and seeing the kitchen. Genevieve put some kind of a powder into Claire's tea. Then she picked up a pillow, and in it she placed----she placed..."

"This," Jane produced the figure.

"Take it away! Take it away!" Laurel screamed.

"I'm sorry. I didn't mean..."

"Burn it, Jane," Eva commanded. "Take it to the fireplace and burn it now."

"What is that thing?" Laurel asked.

"As I told you, I believe Doctor James knew that Genevieve was practicing voodoo. One way to place a spell on someone is to do what you saw Genevieve do in your vision. Often times the practitioner would make a fetish and place it in the pillow of the person who was the object of the spell."

"Who put it in my bedroom, Eva, and why?"

"I think you're getting too close to the secrets of Belle Rouge."

By the time Jane returned to the room, Laurel had settled down. "I have something else to tell you," she said. "When Beth left on Christmas Eve, she lied about going to her father's. She's at Lucien Caulder's."

"Oh no. Surely not," Eva exclaimed.

"Yes. I saw them together."

"He's an evil man," Jane said. "He's cruel and evil. He hurts everyone he touches."

"He's hurt you badly, too. Hasn't he?" Laurel sympathized.

"Yes. More than anyone knows," came the reply.

"Laurel, why don't you get some rest now?"

"I don't want to sleep, Eva. Will both of you stay with me awhile? I want to know more of what you've learned. Jane, did you find anything to verify your dreams?"

"Yes. The clerk at the Miller Hotel kept very lengthy notes. Preston was at the Lennox Hotel visiting Alexandra a couple of months before the Cup race."

"Do you know the date of the race, Jane?" Laurel asked.

"The researcher found the records kept by the racing officials. Among the entries were a mare from Tennessee; Scarlet Satan, owned by S. Kilgore; and Shadow Dancer, owned by Preston Miller and ridden by a D. la Claire." Jane smiled. "I think Alexandra couldn't resist naming her 'French' jockey la Claire."

"And from my dream," Laurel added, "I know Doctor James was right to assume Genevieve was using some of her pagan rituals on Claire."

"Whatever she used, it was working on Claire's mind," Eva said. "You must not go back to that house, Laurel."

"I have to. I have to finish my book."

"Not right now. You can stay here with me while the water damage is repaired."

"Oh, I left the faucet running, didn't I? I bet it's a mess. Do you think you could put up with me for a few days?"

"Of course. You get some rest. I'll see Jane out."

Jane slid under the steering wheel. Before she fastened the seatbelt, she reached into her coat pocket, pulled out the fetish and smoothed its feathers.

Eva took a quilt out of the closet and covered Laurel. "It's going to be cold tonight. You'll probably need this."

"I must have looked pretty stupid tonight sitting in that corner."

"Just frightened. But remember, voodoo only works if you believe it does."

"Eva, I don't want you to think I'm a raving idiot. It's just that when I was little I was playing under a tree in the yard. My mother told me that a bird had a nest in a tree. I just got too close. I looked up in time to see the bird attacking. Its beak and talons----dear God, I still can't bear the thought of it."

"And the fetish brought those feelings back," Eva said. "Does it resemble what you saw Genevieve put in the pillow? And where did you find it?"

"It's the same. I found it when I was getting some clothes out of the dresser drawer. Something pricked my finger. When I took the thing out, I saw what it was and I guess I blacked out for a while. I don't remember anything else till I woke up here."

"Well, you don't have to worry about it any more," Eva assured her. It's burned."

The next morning, Laurel awoke from a restless sleep. Her dreams had been incessant, but in the light of morning their memory quickly faded.

Soon, Eva was at the bedroom door with a breakfast tray. "Did you sleep well?" she asked.

"Yes, I did. But you didn't need to go to all this trouble. I could have gotten up."

"No trouble. I like having someone in the house. Would you rather eat alone?"

"Please sit down. I can tell there's something on your mind."

"See there," Eva smiled. "You're beginning to use your perception."

"I certainly didn't use it where Beth and Lucien were concerned."

"I didn't see it coming either."

A sudden chill made Laurel pull the covers tighter around her. “It’s unbelievable they would be together. He’s old enough to be her father.”

“That may be the very reason she’s attracted to him,” Eva replied. “In a sense, she’s lost her father to a new woman. Maybe Lucien is his replacement.”

“What can I do to get her away from him?”

“Very little, I’m afraid. Whatever you’d do, she’d interpret as jealously. Besides, she’s over twenty-one.”

Laurel blinked back tears. “Beth has always tried to do things to hurt me, and now she has done the ultimate. My daughter is sleeping with a man I’ve made love to. I can’t bear to think of it.”

“Were you in love with Lucien Caulder?”

“No!” Laurel shot back.

“Then your main concern is that your daughter’s with a dangerous man. Laurel, I’m going to stick my nose in your business. After I’ve had my say, you can tell me to butt out. Beth isn’t your enemy. She’s not your rival. She’s a child who needs guidance and love from her mother. Talk to her?”

“Oh, I’m sure all I have to do is phone over there and she’ll jump at the chance of hearing my voice.”

Eva sighed. “Just remember, you have a choice to make. Which is worse? Swallowing your pride or leaving your daughter with Lucien.”

“Will you go with me to talk to her, Eva?”

“I’ll set up a meeting with Beth right away.”

Few customers were in the Town Cafe, when Eva and Beth met there in midafternoon. They sat in a corner booth, and with no mention of Lucien Caulder, the conversation was pleasant until Beth spotted Laurel.

“Did you set me up for this, Eva?” she asked.

"You and your mother have a few things to discuss."

"My mother has never been able to discuss anything. She lectures."

"If you don't owe it to her to listen, you do owe it to yourself. Don't drive her away. A mother is a hard thing to be without."

"I wish you were my mother, Eva."

Laurel slid in the seat across from Beth. "I'm glad you came."

Beth looked away. "I wouldn't have if I'd known you were going to be here."

"I know," Laurel replied. "But don't blame Eva. She only wanted to help."

"I realize that."

"I don't know where to begin, Beth. I rehearsed and rehearsed what I wanted to say, and now nothing seems right."

"That's a first---my mother being at a loss for words."

"Perhaps I should just say that if Lucien Caulder makes you happy, then I give you my blessings. I don't intend to interfere with your life. You're free to make your own choices."

Laurel stood up to go. "Just remember, you're welcome at Belle Rouge anytime."

Beth watched her mother as she crossed the street and got into her truck. "Well," she said, "I never expected her to say that."

"Your mother's trying to change."

"It certainly was a change for her to say I was free to make my own choices."

"But there is a certain responsibility with that freedom, Beth. You have to accept the consequences of your decisions."

# CHAPTER 13

Laurel awakened at 2 am. For an hour she tossed and turned, then she fell into a light sleep and began to dream. She drove south out of Louisville toward Cedarville. Her agent sat beside her. "Not what you expected?" she asked.

"You mean that you live in the boonies? Nah, I'm not surprised. I always suspected you were a borderline eccentric."

Laurel smiled at him. "How did you like the chapters of 'The Secrets of Cedarville' I sent you?"

"That's why I came. I showed them to the producer of "Beyond Revelation." Hell, you struck some kind of a chord with her. She told me to get my butt here and pick up the rest of the book. She's gung ho. She's not only going to be very involved with the screenplay, she's going to direct the movie. This movie may even be released before your first one."

The agent leaned forward in his seat as they turned into the drive. "Good grief! So this is Belle Rouge. No wonder your writing has taken such a turn. This place is creepy."

Laurel glanced toward the glass room. "It can be."

They were settled into the study when the agent asked, "Is your 'Cedarville' manuscript ready for me to take back to California?"

"No," Laurel replied.

"But the note you sent me said you had only a couple more chapters to write. Why haven't you finished it?"

"I can't. I--I haven't been feeling well."

"You sure as hell better get well. I have to leave day after tomorrow with the final chapters in hand."

"That's impossible. I've been away from home for two weeks while some plumbing problems were repaired. I just got back in yesterday."

"Laurel Mackenzie," the agent pointed his finger, "all I can tell you is I'm not going into the producer's office and tell her you haven't finished the book because of plumbing problems. You don't do that to Nila Castile. She eats people alive."

"I don't think I can finish the book at all. This writing is doing something to me."

"Ah, come on. This isn't your first book. You know better than to get sucked into your story."

"This is different," Laurel replied.

The agent watched Laurel's face for any change in expression. "Castile will hire someone else to finish it. Do you want that?"

"She wouldn't dare."

"The hell she wouldn't. I know her. She wants this book. You have two days to come up with something." The agent rose to his feet. "Take me to a motel. I'm tired."

"Oh no," Laurel said. "You'll stay here. I wouldn't think of your staying anywhere else."

"Is this my punishment for scolding you---to sleep in a haunted house?" he asked. "All right. I'll stay. Bring on the ghosts of Lily and Sumner."

He followed Laurel upstairs. "You don't need to experience Lily or Sumner," she smiled. "I think Claire's room is the most suitable. This is where she was entertaining Philippe Dumont the night Sumner confronted them. Yes, this is the room where you should sleep."

Laurel started to leave, but she stopped at the doorway. "By the way, did you say Ms. Castile's first name is Nila?"

Eva arrived within minutes of receiving Laurel's call. "What happened?" she asked, throwing her coat across the kitchen chair.

"Two things. Beth came home last night, and I had a most vivid dream."

"Oh," Eva released a sigh of relief. "I'm so glad Beth came to her senses. What prompted her to leave Lucien?"

"It was Lucien's idea. I thought at first he'd simply grown tired of her, or perhaps he felt he'd succeeded at getting back at me. But I didn't question. I let her volunteer. Yesterday morning, Lucien found a fetish in the shape of a bird on his pillow when he awoke. Beth said it was evident he was very disturbed. Lucien told her to leave for her own safety."

"What's wrong?" Laurel questioned when she saw the look on Eva's face.

"I thought it might be Lucien who put the fetish in your room, to scare you. But evidently it wasn't."

"What else, Eva? Talk to me."

"I told Jane to burn the fetish, and now it reappears at Lucien's house."

"You don't think she was the one who put it in my house. Do you? Why would she do such a thing?"

Eva grabbed her coat. "I don't know, but we're going to find out. Leave Beth a note. Let's pay Jane a visit."

When they arrived at Jane's house a sheriff's car was parked in the driveway. Eva pulled in beside it, and she and Laurel got out.

"John," Eva called. "What's happened?"

"A little accident. Jane fell down the stairs. Said she slipped on something."

"Is she all right?" Laurel asked.

"She has some bad bruises and maybe a broken arm. The ambulance took her to the hospital."

"We should go there right away," Eva exclaimed.

"I'm off duty in an hour," the deputy said. "If you'd like to wait, I'll drive you in."

"No, John. I'm going on. Could you take Laurel home?"

"Sure, Eva. I'll be happy to." The deputy turned toward Laurel and offered his hand. I'm John Miller, Jane's cousin."

He opened the car door for Laurel. She studied Miller as he walked around to driver's side. He was tall and thin, but his tight shirt revealed muscular shoulders. He was blond, like Jane and when he took off his hat and pitched it in the back seat, she noticed his hair line was beginning to recede.

His smile told her he had noticed she was staring. She knew she was blushing. "Everything OK?" he asked.

"It's just that I've never ridden in a police car before," Laurel responded.

"Oh," John Miller smiled again and started the car. He said nothing more until they pulled onto the main road. "So you're THE Laurel Mackenzie."

"Yes, I am."

"I've read all your books."

"They tell me mostly women read them."

"Which is supposed to mean what, Ms. Mackenzie?"

"You needn't be defensive, Mr. Miller. It doesn't mean a thing."

"I think it might be you who's defensive."

Laurel stared straight ahead, not daring to look at him. "I thought you were a deputy sheriff, not a psychologist."

"You're good," Miller grinned.

"You have no idea how good I am." Stunned at her own reply, Laurel glanced his way. "I'm sorry, I didn't mean 'good' in that way."

The deputy roared with laughter. "In a sexual way? Sometimes you catch yourself in your own trap, don't you?"

"You're good too. I mean---I mean---" Laurel blushed again.

"---at word games," he finished her sentence. "We're both good at word games."

"Yes. My daughter says I do it all the time."

"That's the girl who was with Lucien Caulder?"

"Word gets around fast," Laurel sighed.

"It does when you live in a small town, Ms. Mackenzie."

"How well do you know Lucien?" she asked.

"I've known him all my life."

"Tell me about him."

"He's always been a loner---manages to hurt people who get too close. I know he hurt Jane badly."

Laurel shifted her weight in the seat. "Mr. Miller, may I confide in you, not as a police officer, but, as a friend of Jane's."

John Miller's incredibly blue eyes stared directly into hers and he nodded.

Laurel related the story of the fetish and how Eva had told Jane to burn it. But now it had mysteriously shown up again at Lucien Caulder's. "I'm not placing blame, Mr. Miller. I'm worried about what's been happening since I moved to Belle Rouge."

"What else happened? Things that should have been reported to the police?"

"I told you I don't want to talk to a police officer. I want to talk to a friend."

John turned into the drive at Belle Rouge. His voice softened. "I want to be your friend, Laurel."

"Thanks," she said. "If you have time to come in, I'll fix breakfast to pay you back for the ride home."

"I don't need any payback, but I am hungry." He glanced at his watch. "Thirty minutes to go on my shift."

"It'll take me that long to cook something. You go ahead and play policeman. Look around the barn. You can say I asked you to investigate a prowler or something. By that time breakfast will be ready."

"Sounds good. I suppose you'd be offended if I came around and opened the car door for you."

Not at all," Laurel grinned. "Here's the key to the back door. You can open that for me, too."

Laurel followed the deputy up the walk. He unlocked the door and held it open. He made no attempt to step back, and Laurel's body touched his as she tried to pass.

"Your keys," he said, stopping her in front of him. "From your back door man," he winked.

His hand closed around hers in a gentle caress as she took the keys. "You can come in the front door any time," she said. She forced herself to look away. "Go!" she said. "Go check the barn or something."

"Yes ma'am." John Miller gave her a mock salute and headed off toward the barn.

Laurel watched him till he reached the gate. He turned back and gave her another smile.

When she entered the kitchen she found a note on the table.

*Mom,* it read, *Eva phoned and said Jane would be in the hospital overnight. Hope you don't mind, but I took the car. I need to get out of the house. Thought I'd go see her.*

*Love, Beth*

Laurel was putting breakfast on the table when John returned. “Well, did you find anything suspicious?” she asked.

“Nope.” He sat down where Laurel pointed. “Just saw some good-looking horses. They belong to Allen Williams. Don’t they?”

“Doesn’t anything escape you, Deputy? I know----Cedarville is a small town.”

“In my line of work, you have to observe everything,” he said.

“You aren’t exactly what I would picture as a typical small town cop. I would almost say---a teacher, like Jane, or certainly some kind of a white collar professional, not a blue...”

“My collar is brown, Miss MacKenzie, or haven’t you noticed the uniform?”

“I didn’t mean anything derogatory. Why would you take offense?”

John Miller rearranged the scrambled eggs on his plate. Finally he answered. “You hit a sore spot with me.”

“In what way?” Laurel asked.

“The college thing, I guess.”

“Oh, you didn’t get to go?”

“I went for a year and dropped out to get married.”

“I see.” Laurel sat back in her chair. “You had to go to work to support your family.”

“My wife was a few years older than I. She had a good job. Guess I didn’t want to be supported by her. I took a job at a factory, but the government rescued me. A few months after we married, I was in Vietnam. It doesn’t make a lot of sense. A green nineteen-year-old who’d done nothing more dangerous than mow a lawn, was given a gun and told to kill people.”

"That had to be quite a shock. How did you manage to survive?"

"The main question you ask yourself after a while is not how, but why. Why did I make it and my buddies didn't?"

"I hear men in combat try not to make friends."

"An eighteen-year-old doesn't realize that, Miss MacKenzie. He's away from home for the first time, needing friends. Then he watches as they're blown to bits in front of his eyes."

Laurel found it increasingly difficult to swallow her food. She pushed the plate away. "I can see why you'd go into your line of work. Now you can protect people."

"It wasn't that noble. The job was available. I didn't need much money to live on. My wife didn't stick around, you see. She went off with a 'white collar' man---her divorce lawyer."

"Do you still love her."

"No," Miller laughed. "I was never in love with her."

"That's an easy defense, John. Convincing yourself you never loved someone helps to bury the pain."

"Maybe," he said. "It's more likely those years in Nam taught the nineteen-year-old to keep his distance."

"That's not what I felt from you when you were standing in my doorway a few minutes ago."

"That was sexual, Miss MacKenzie, purely sexual."

Laurel picked up the plates and took them to the sink. "I see," she said.

She could sense he was behind her. He reached around her and placed the cups on top of the plates. Then his arms slipped around her waist. She turned to face him. His lips gently touched hers. "You're right," she whispered. "Purely sexual."

## CHAPTER 14

Eva sat beside Jane's bed at the hospital, but Jane faced away from her. "You might as well talk to me."

"I don't have anything to say," Jane replied.

Eva touched her shoulder. "Just tell me this. Did you put the fetish on Laurel's pillow?"

"No! I wouldn't do that."

"Then why did you put it in Lucien's house?"

Jane released a sighed. "I wanted to scare him. He's very superstitious. When I saw how he hurt Laurel by using her daughter, I had to make him stop."

"All of this has brought back a lot of memories, hasn't it?"

Jane nodded and turned away again.

"Do you want to talk about it? You know what you say will go no further."

"I know," Jane sobbed.

Eva moved to the chair on the opposite side of the bed so Jane could keep her back to the hospital room door. "I've always known you were carrying a burden that you never shared. It would lighten a bit if you told someone."

Jane took the tissue Eva offered. "You remember we didn't keep track of one another when I went off to college. It was a lonely time for me---first time away from home, no friends, except one."

"Who was that?" Eva frowned.

"I never had the money to come home on the weekends, but I wasn't at school either. Lucien came to visit me. The first time he came into town, he said he was there on business and just decided to phone the dorm. I was lonely, and he reminded me of home."

"I wondered why you were engaged to him so quickly when you came home that first summer," Eva said. "You'd already been seeing him for almost a year."

"The romance lasted through my sophomore year," Jane continued, "but then something happened."

"You transferred to another college. In fact, you went directly into summer school."

"No, I didn't," Jane sobbed. "I---I was pregnant. I had to leave my first college. I couldn't hide the pregnancy any longer."

"You were engaged. Why didn't you and Lucien get married?"

"He didn't want children, so he wouldn't marry me. There was no summer school. I stayed with my cousin in Savannah, Georgia, until the baby was born. In late July I had a girl. Then I enrolled in another college in September."

"You had the baby? Where is it?"

"I don't know. I have never known! They let me hold her. I nursed her, and then they took her from me to give to some family."

Eva gathered Jane in her arms. "Oh no. Why did they let you do that? How could anyone be so cruel?"

Lucien Caulder stared at the fetish on the table in front of him. "It's been a long time since I've seen the likes of you." He took a pencil and turned it over. "Where the hell did you come from?"

A rapping on the back door startled him. Delicately he picked up the fetish and placed it in a cabinet drawer. "Damn!" he said when he saw John Miller standing on the stoop.

He half opened the door. "What do you want?"

"Let me in, Lucien. I have some questions for you."

"I was just leaving."

Miller pushed his way inside. "Not till we talk."

Lucien motioned for the deputy to sit down. "I'll stand," he said.

"Suit yourself. Make this quick. I have to be somewhere in a few minutes."

"Jane fell down her stairway this morning. What do you know about it?"

"What do you mean? How could I know anything about it?"

John leaned back against the counter and crossed his arms. "She said she heard some noise downstairs, and when she started down to investigate she felt someone push her."

"You think I was in her house? What reason would I have?"

"That's what I'm asking."

Lucien stopped directly in front of the deputy. "I've had nothing to do with that woman for years. Besides, I have a witness who will place me here, in my bed till midmorning. She'll vouch for me. It's Laurel Mackenzie's daughter," he grinned. "I'm sure you can find her at Belle Rouge. Now, get out. I have to go."

John stopped just outside the door. "Stay away from Jane," he warned. "You've hurt her enough."

"Why so testy, John?" Lucien called after him. "Maybe you ought to have something new in your bed. It helps take the edge off. Laurel's not bad. Help yourself, I'm through with her."

Laurel sat down at the typewriter and placed her fingers on the keys. "I just can't do it," she said angrily. "I can't write."

She pushed her chair away from the desk. "Maybe my dream concerning my agent was a prophecy," she thought. "Maybe he will come here and demand the manuscript I can't produce."

She got up, went to the kitchen and fixed herself a cup of tea. "With all this pressure I feel, I can see why I'd dream about my agent. But why did I insist he sleep in Claire's room? And why are the movie producer and woman on the plane both named Nila?"

Laurel ambled back toward the den. "What do I do with myself for the rest of the day? I can't write---maybe I should read."

She chose a novel at random from the bookcase and plopped down on the couch. Her mind drifted to John Miller. She could feel him. She could smell his cologne. It was still on her clothing. What was it about him that attracted her so, she wondered. Animalistic. That's what it had to be. Purely animalistic.

Absentmindedly she leafed through the book. "No," she concluded, there was something more here than sexual attraction. She actually felt she had known him for a very long time.

John Miller sat in a corner booth at the empty Towne Cafe, ignoring the cold cup of coffee in front of him. "I have no business getting involved with her," he said to himself, not if I want to run for sheriff. A campaign will take all the extra time I have."

He pulled a pack of cigarettes out of his coat pocket, lit one and took a long draw. The smoke was choking, and he quickly crushed the cigarette in the ashtray. "Why would I think I could have a good relationship with her anyway? None of the rest of them have been very successful."

He had thought about his past relationships a lot lately, wondering why he could never seem to make a commitment, at least emotionally, to any woman. Perhaps it went back to Vietnam. Everything always did. At least that's what the psychologist at the hospital where he recuperated had told him.

"You were very young when you went to Vietnam," the doctor had said. "Your first experience came with women who were readily available and who offered nothing more than a quick sexual fix. That formed your pattern of relationships."

John Miller stared into the curl of smoke rising from the ashes of the cigarette. Another quick fix. Is that what he wanted from Laurel Mackenzie?

The image of Lucien Caulder touching her formed in his mind. He got up and threw some money on the table. No, Lucien," he thought. "I'm not going to take my turn with her."

Laurel heard the knob turn on the front door. "Beth, is that you?"

"Yes, Mom. Where are you?"

"In the den."

"Are you busy?" Beth asked.

"No. I can't write. Come in and sit down."

Laurel watched as her daughter lay back in the lounge chair. "You don't look like you feel very well. Are you all right?"

"Yes," Beth averted her gaze. "I didn't see Jane."

"Oh?"

"I just drove around."

"Sometimes I do that, too," Laurel smiled.

"Mom, why aren't you angry with me about Lucien?"

"There's no point in being angry. I've been angry all my life, and I'm just now realizing it."

Beth managed a feeble smile. "I think Cedarville's been good for you."

"It's had a curious effect, almost like a catalyst to change my life. I'd even started to write again. It was flowing from me. But it's stopped."

"Why's that?"

"I've lost touch with the characters."

"Eva believes you sometimes get too closely involved with them."

"I've been told that."

"She's very worried about you, Mom. She told me how she found you with the fetish. She described seeing you in the glass room. And who is the old black man that no one else has seen?"

"Writers have to have vivid imaginations, Beth."

"Is Barney a figment of your imagination?"

"It's possible that Eva doesn't know everyone in Cedarville."

"I suppose so," Beth shrugged.

"Are you hungry?" Laurel asked. "You want something to eat?"

"No, my stomach's been a little upset."

"Then you're sick?"

"I think it's just my nerves, Mom."

"Lucien can have that effect on people," Laurel responded.

Beth fiddled with the button on her sweater. "He told me about your affair with him."

"Why am I not surprised?"

"He's cruel, Mom."

"I know."

"Why was I so stupid?"

"Come here, honey."

Beth curled up beside Laurel and placed her head on her Mother's shoulder.

Laurel brushed the hair back from her daughter's face. "We've all done stupid things in our lives. I'm angry with myself for getting involved with him." She took Beth's face in her hands. "But if it took the experience with Lucien Caulder for us to be able to have this talk, it was worth it."

## CHAPTER 15

The next few weeks moved by slowly for Laurel. Beth left for North Carolina to see her father, and Eva devoted her time to Jane. Twice Laurel had seen John Miller on the street in Cedarville, but he hadn't noticed her, or he was purposely ignoring her. He had every reason to avoid her, she thought. She'd been terribly forward with him the day he brought her home from Jane's.

Laurel finally gave up trying to finish her novel. The wastebasket held all her feeble attempts. She'd even retraced her steps since coming to Cedarville, trying to get back into the flow. She went to the sale barn and her own barn, where she and Barney had found Claire's box. She went to the glass room. None of the creative energy remained in those places. It was as if the story of Belle Rouge had died.

On this particular day she was rereading Sumner Kilgore's words from her last written chapter. *"Do you see this woman, Claire? Do you see that pitiful child she's carrying in her arms? If you had continued with Philippe Dumont, this is what you would look like one year from now. Scream all you want, daughter, but I have saved you from this horrible fate. Go ahead, Claire. Scream!"*

Suddenly, it dawned on Laurel. "I can't write because I haven't experienced Claire's pain. It was not ordinary pain. It was excruciating. It was the pain of being betrayed by both her father and her lover. I don't know those feelings."

The knocking broke her thoughts. "Oh, this is a surprise," she said as she opened the door. "I thought you were trying to avoid me."

Deputy Miller took off his hat and came in. "I've been busy."

"I read in the paper you've announced your candidacy for sheriff. Following in Preston's footsteps, I guess."

John ignored Laurel's remark and handed her a thick folder. "Jane wanted me to loan this to you. They're Preston's notes and some of his papers from the hotel. I've picked out the ones that mention Alexandra Lennox."

"Did those two have an affair?" Laurel asked.

"It's possible, but I believe he thought she was too far above his reach---class wise, I mean."

"Oh, I see. Is that belief something you also share with Preston Miller?"

The deputy sat down on the couch and removed his dark glasses. "I'm not afraid of you, if that's what you mean."

Laurel sat down beside him. "Oh really?"

"No," he smiled, taking her in his arms. "I carry a gun."

Eva fluffed the pillow and placed it behind Jane's back. "I'm not an invalid," Jane said. "You're the one who needs to get some rest. You've been over here every day for two weeks. Besides, it's time I fend for myself."

"You're still weak, and your injuries aren't causing it. You've had the classic symptoms of shock. I think you saw who pushed you down the stairs."

"I realize I've tried to block it out of my mind, but it's been coming back. All I remember is, dark hair."

"Was it Lucien Caulder?"

"I thought so at first. I thought he was getting back at me for putting the fetish in his house. But now I'm sure it was a woman, with long black hair."

"Have you told John what you remember?"

"No. We talk about Preston and Alexandra---and Laurel."

"Laurel?" Eva asked. "Why her?"

"Remember, we had just starting talking about Preston and Alexandra's deal with the horses when I fell. John has Preston's papers, so I asked him to take them to Laurel. Maybe reading them will help her get back to her writing."

Eva frowned. "I wouldn't encourage him to go around her if I were you."

"Why would you say a thing like that, Eva Farnsworth?"

"The day you had your accident, you didn't see the way they looked at each other."

"You mean----? But you know it's not possible for something to get started with them. It just can't."

Laurel and John made passionate love. He knew how to touch her, gently. He knew how to fulfill her. "Who taught him?" she wondered. She didn't care, she convinced herself. It was she who was the beneficiary of that teacher.

They lay quietly against one another. "You're not going to run away, now?" she asked.

He kissed her forehead. "I have a few more minutes. I have some work to do."

"Have you slept since your shift ended?"

He shook his head.

"Then sleep here. I'll fix dinner for us tonight."

John threw back the covers. "No, I can't do that. I really do have work to attend to."

"All right." Laurel put on her robe. "But I'd like to go over Preston's papers with you."

"Why don't you type them onto your computer? We can look at them tomorrow."

"I don't have a computer, John."

"It would be much easier for you to write if you had one."

"I wouldn't know what kind to get."

"If you'd like, I'll go with you to buy one. That is, if you'd care to."

"If you show me how to use it," Laurel grinned. "It might take a while," Laurel smiled.

He kissed her once again. "I'll find the time."

John Miller came to Belle Rouge every day during the next week. He set up the computer Laurel had purchased, and coached her through the word processing program.

Eva called several times asking about Preston's papers, but she was not asked to come to Belle Rouge. Laurel explained to her how busy she was and that she felt, with the computer, her writing process would be more efficient.

"Then you are writing," Eva said.

"Not yet, but I will be soon," Laurel replied.

John and Laurel soon fell into a pattern. He would come to Belle Rouge in the mornings, just as he got off work. They would make love, and he would be gone by noon.

He had just left one morning, when Laurel went to the barn to feed. Allen Williams found her there.

"The black mare's supposed to foal first," he said.

"I'll keep close watch on her," Laurel replied. "Not like I did my mare."

"What happened to your mare wasn't your fault. She jumped the fence and broke her back."

"It doesn't make any sense to me that she'd do that. She'd never jumped a fence before."

"Maybe something scared her," Williams offered.

"That's what I believe," Laurel agreed. "but what could have scared her that badly?"

"We may never know the answer. But let me give you some good news. I'm going to run Red Satan next week at Keeneland."

"You think he's ready?"

"We'll see. If he comes out all right, I'll run him at Churchill next month."

"That is good news. I'm thrilled."

"I'm going to unload this feed and get back to the training center."

As Williams dumped the grain into the bin, Laurel gathered the empty feed bags and rolled them together. "Does Lucien still have his horse at Hickory Ridge?" she asked. "We haven't seen him for about a week. Karen's been feeding his horse."

It was early evening when Lucien Caulder's car turned onto River Street. He drove down the narrow street and past the small, odd-shaped houses which hung precariously on the riverbank. At the dead end, near the graveyard, he got out and made his way to the last house.

It was evident no one had lived there for quite some time. Vandals had left an old mattress in the corner of the front room, and tin cans were everywhere.

Lucien went to the blackened fireplace and removed a brick on the right side. He pulled the fetish from his pocket, put it inside the compartment and replaced the brick.

"It will be mine. I promise you that," he said out loud.

He didn't hear the approaching footsteps. "Caulder! What are you doing here?"

Lucien whirled around to see John Miller standing in the doorway. He collected himself before he spoke. "On duty early, aren't you, deputy."

"Yes, I am. Why are you prowling around?"

"It is my property."

"Not any more. You sold it to the city."

"Maybe I just needed to see the old home place one more time. What are they going to do with it?"

"Burn it next week."

"Good," Lucien smiled. "I think I'll come watch it. It holds nothing for me anymore."

Laurel talked Eva into accompanying her to Keeneland. They were crossing the river bridge when they noticed the smoke. "Wonder what's burning?" Laurel asked.

"Looks to me like it might be Lucien Caulder's old home place. I heard the city bought it and was going to get rid of it. They must have decided to give the fire department a little practice."

Laurel headed the car for the interstate. "I don't picture Lucien coming from such a poor area," she said.

"His family was poor all right. The lack of money has grieved him all his life. He had absolutely nothing when we were in high school."

Laurel put the car on cruise and settled back. "I think it still bothers him. What does he live on?"

"He had a civilian job at the army post and retired on disability."

"Well, let's not spend this beautiful day talking about Lucien," Laurel said. "We're on our way to Keeneland to watch Red Satan win his first race. I'm so happy you could come with me, Eva. I've missed you since you've been taking care of Jane."

"I wasn't sure I should leave her, but she insisted."

"I wanted her to come with us, too. Why wouldn't she?"

Eva adjusted the sun visor. "She still doesn't have her strength back."

"It's been weeks since her accident. Is something else wrong besides her broken arm?"

"She's ashamed she put the fetish in Lucien's house. She was trying to scare him." Something stopped Eva from telling Laurel that Jane knew someone pushed her down the stairs. "I just think a lot of things caught up to her at one time and put her under a lot of stress. She's much better though. We may go visit her cousin in Savannah soon. Maybe you could come with us?"

"I doubt I can. Have you ever been to Savannah before?"

"No, but Jane lived there with her cousin one summer while she was in college. Have you been there?"

"Not that I remember," Laurel smiled. "My parents lived there when I was born."

## CHAPTER 16

Keeneland Race Course was small and quaint in comparison to Churchill Downs. Located just outside Lexington, and made of wood and stone, it blended harmoniously with the beautiful rolling countryside. There wasn't even a public address system to invade the idyllic setting.

The crowd was small this weekday, so Laurel and Eva sat in the grandstand just opposite finish line.

"How does it feel to see your horse's name in the racing form?" Eva asked. "Look. Race number one, Maiden--Purse $20,650, for 2-year-olds."

Laurel beamed as she saw the words printed on the page, Crimson Lion---Ch. c. 2, by Stealthy Lion-Red Lady, by Crimson Satan; Br.-Crit Sargent; Tr.-Allen Williams; Own.-Belle Rouge Farm" "I can't believe it. It's a dream come true," Laurel said. "Let's go to the stable area and see how things are going."

As they walked beneath the grandstand, Laurel glanced at the TV monitor. Across the screen came the changes for the first race. "Eva, look! Crimson Lion's been scratched. "What could be wrong?"

"Laurel, Laurel!" Allen Williams called from across the saddling ring.

"What is it, what happened?" she asked.

"I'm not sure," Williams shook his head, "but Lion's left front ankle is swollen, and it has quite a bit of heat in it. It's probably not serious, but I think we'd better check it out before we run him."

"Oh great!" Laurel fought back the tears. "What else is going to happen to my horses?" Sometimes I think Sumner Kilgore's luck is following me."

"We'll win another day," Allen insisted. "Just give me a little time to check the horse out."

"I know you're right. I'm glad you noticed the problem before Lion injured himself even more."

"Actually, it wasn't me who noticed it. Karen and I stepped away from the stall for a couple of minutes to get some supplies from the truck, and when we got back, a woman was standing there looking at the horse. She was the one who called my attention to Lion's ankle."

"We should be grateful to her," Laurel said.

"Maybe," Eva frowned. "Do you think she could have done something to Lion? Did you get her name?"

"She told me, but I don't recall. I think it started with an N. We were away from the stall a couple of minutes. And if she had done something to him, she wouldn't have pointed it out."

"That's probably true," Laurel replied.

"Well," Allen sighed, "I think scratching Lion was the best thing to do. I wasn't happy with the jockey we had anyway. Next time, I'm going to use an apprentice I just met. His name's MacCallum. He's fresh over from Sussex, England, and he's eager to please. I didn't like the way this race was shaping up either. It's probably too short a distance for Lion, and there's a lot of speed in it. At least four of the entries are speed horses. I don't believe there's any way he would have had time to catch the front runners. I imagine the best he could do would be to finish somewhere in the middle of the pack. Lion's going to do better at Churchill where the races are longer."

Laurel and Eva were already on the Interstate when Laurel turned on the radio to catch the call of the first race.

*...and as they reach the head of the stretch, it's Hurricane Bay with a slight lead. On the inside, Gold Meridian looks for racing room. In the middle of the track, Doomsday and Idlewild are moving together. Then it's a gap of three lengths where April Dahlia leads the tightly bunched field. As they approach the sixteenth pole Gold Meridian sticks his nose in front.*

*Oh Oh! April Dahlia's gone down! Boswain is unable to avoid him. Altaview has unseated his rider!"*

"That could have been Lion," Laurel cried. If he had run in the middle of the pack like Allen said he would, he would have been involved in that accident!"

Deputy Miller spotted Lucien Caulder's car heading south out of Cedarville. His instinct told him to follow. When Caulder turned into the drive of Belle Rouge, Miller pulled onto the side road just opposite. He drove to the top of the hill, where he could see the entire layout of the farm.

He watched as Lucien received no response to his knock. When Caulder got back in his car, he proceeded toward the barn. He disappeared into the stable area for a few seconds, then reappeared and started across the back field. The deputy took out his binoculars. Caulder was headed for the Kilgore family graveyard.

Jane stirred from her afternoon nap. Her dream remained vivid. Quickly she reached into the nightstand, took out a notebook and pen and began to write.

*I walked toward my cousin's house in Savannah. No one else was on the street. As I rounded the corner, I came in full view of the front of the house. A tall dark woman was coming out. She held something in her arms. (I think it was a baby---my baby). There was someone parked in a car in front of the house. The tall dark woman handed the baby to the person in the car. As the car drove off I saw that the tall dark woman had a briefcase in her hand. The initial "N" was on the briefcase.*

It was late afternoon when Laurel and Eva arrived back at Cedarville. Laurel saw two familiar cars parked in front of the Town Cafe. "Look who's there---John and Lucien," she said.

"Wonder what's going on," Eva frowned.

"I'm sure it's just a coincidence," Laurel replied. "Do you want to go home, or do you want to come out to Belle Rouge for a while?"

"Take me on to my house. I think I'll give Jane a call."

When Laurel reached the farm, some thirty minutes later, she could see John Miller's car by the back door. He got out when she pulled in beside him.

"How did your horse do?" he asked.

"Allen scratched him. There's something wrong with his ankle. It was a trip for nothing." Miller followed her into the kitchen. "Want something to drink?" she asked.

"No," I'm here on business. "Do you have any idea why Lucien Caulder would be interested in the Kilgore graveyard?"

"Heavens no!"

"I saw him here earlier today, and I just confronted him. He said he was looking for you and thought you might be in the back field when he didn't find you at the house or the barn."

"How did you come to see him?"

"I followed him here."

Laurel smiled. "Are you jealous?"

"This isn't a joke," the deputy snapped.

"I see it's not. Why do you think he was here?"

Miller chose his words carefully. "I think he's looking for something. I caught him rummaging through his family's homeplace on the river, too."

"Now he knows you're following him," Laurel added. "I'm sure he doesn't like that."

"He certainly doesn't. But I want him to know I'm on to him."

"There's more to your acquaintance with Lucien than you're saying. Isn't there?"

John Miller slumped into a chair. "I despise him for what he's done to Jane."

"Is there something more than a broken engagement?"

"Much more."

"Can you tell me?"

"Jane doesn't know I'm aware of the situation." The deputy paused. "Will you promise not to speak to Jane about it unless she brings it up?"

Laurel sat down opposite him. "Of course."

"Jane was pregnant with Lucien's baby, and he wouldn't marry her. She had the baby at our cousin's in Savannah and it was adopted there."

"She and Eva are talking about going to Savannah, and they've asked me to come along," Laurel said. "Do you think she might try to find the child?"

"I don't keep in touch with our cousin. I didn't think Jane did either. But you may be right. Our cousin is elderly, and she's the only one who could tell Jane anything about the baby's whereabouts."

"Does Eva know?"

"I have a feeling she does," Miller replied.

Eva sat in Jane's living room and listened as she related her latest dream. Eva's eyes remained closed in a deep concentration until Jane mentioned the briefcase.

"Repeat that last part," Eva commanded.

"The tall dark woman's briefcase had an 'N' on it. What's wrong?"

"Today at Keeneland---the woman who pointed out Laurel's horse's injury---Allen thought her name began with an 'N'."

"Eva!" Jane cried. "I just remembered something Laurel told us. When she was on the plane, coming back from seeing her agent in California, she said she met a mysterious woman who's name was Nila. Remember? She gave her a poem or something."

Eva's eyes widened. "And Laurel had a dream. She dreamed her agent came here to Cedarville to get the book she's writing. He told her that the producer was also going to direct the movie. Her name was Nila Castile! Come on, Jane. We're going to Belle Rouge."

John Miller's car pulled out of Laurel's drive just before Eva turned in. They waved to him. "Something else is going on," Eva said.

When Laurel opened the door, Eva asked point blank, "What's John doing here?"

"Police business," Laurel replied.

"Oh, good," Jane sighed. "I don't think his wife would like him visiting another woman."

## CHAPTER 17

For several days, Laurel had refused to answer the persistent ringing of the phone. John Miller had come twice, but she didn't go to the door. Neither did she respond when Eva came. Laurel repeatedly read the diary and she retreated further and further into Claire's thoughts. She spent her nights in Claire's bedroom listening to the same scene over and over again.

"Philippe, how could you? You said you loved me."

"Oh, that's not all there is to Mr. Dumont's story. Genevieve," Sumner called. Bring in that wretched creature. I was saving this for tomorrow, daughter, but I think now is a perfect time."

"Do you see this woman, Claire? Do you see that pitiful child in her arms? If you had continued with Philippe Dumont, this is how you would have ended up. Scream all you want daughter, but I have saved you from this horrible fate. Go ahead, Claire. Scream!"

Laurel buried her head in the pillow to muffle her own cries. Finally, she fell into an exhausted sleep. When she awoke, the sun was glaring through the window and for the first time in days, she was hungry. Just as she got to the kitchen, she heard a rap on the door. Instead of responding to the urge to retreat into the inner sanctum of the house, she peeked out the window. Barney's old truck was parked in the driveway.

"Howdy, ma'am," he greeted her. "It's gonna be a nice warm day. Thought you might like to start making a door in that fake wall upstairs."

"How did you know I was thinking about that?" Laurel asked.

"You mentioned it to me the last time I was here."

"I don't think so," she said.

"But you do want to find out what's behind that wall. Don't you, ma'am."

"Yes, I do. Do you have the tools we need?"

"There's probably some in the little barn out to the side there. Why don't you fix yourself a bite to eat while I look. Then we'll get started."

With sufficient tools rounded up, Barney and Laurel began making an entryway into the walled-up room.

"My goodness," Laurel exclaimed, "I've never seen so much dust in my life. What kind of plaster is this?"

"In olden days, ma'am, they used to coat these little strips of wood with a mixture of mud and animal hair. You better tie a handkerchief around your nose and mouth."

"My old Hoover will never clean all this up."

"Most likely we're gonna need a Shop-Vac, Miz Mackenzie. Do you have one?"

"No, but I can run into town and get one."

"You want me to go with you?" Barney asked.

"No, stay here and finish the doorway. I'll be back as soon as I can."

Laurel returned in less than an hour. "Barney!" she called from the yard. "Can you come down and help me drag this thing upstairs?"

When there was no answer after the third call, she hurried into the house and up the stairs. "I wonder where he could be. Surely he hasn't hurt himself."

She stumbled across the debris covering the floor. The doorway had been cut, but the dust was still so thick she couldn't see into the secret room. She fanned the dust away and stepped inside.

Barney sat in an old rocking chair, his eyes closed tightly.

"Why didn't you answer me?" Laurel demanded. "Are you sick? What's wrong?"

Without opening his eyes, the old man spoke in a strong, clear voice. "Miss Claire, don't you worry none. I'll take care of the baby. We'll close up this end of the room, put all the stuff in here, and you won't ever have to look at it again."

Hesitantly, Laurel reached for his shoulder. "Barney, it's me, Laurel MacKenzie."

Slowly he opened his eyes. "Whew, I guess it got a little too close in here. I just had to sit down a minute."

"You didn't have to get all this done by yourself. I was going to help you."

"I'm just fine now, ma'am. We better get this stuff cleaned up."

Laurel motioned for Barney to remain in the chair. "Oh, no you don't! First, I want to know more about Claire Kilgore."

"I only know what you told me, ma'am."

"You just said something about her and a baby and closing this room up."

Barney shook his head and laughed. "You young people just gotta forgive the ramblings of us old folks. I dozed off. I was probably dreaming."

"How much do you know about what happened here at Belle Rouge, Barney?"

"Not much, ma'am. Did you finish the diary? I expect it might answer some of your questions."

"Yes, I have. But Claire wrote only a few more passages after her father exposed Philippe Dumont as a scoundrel."

Barney's eyes saddened. "Not surprised. It must hurt a lot when someone you trusted lets you down."

"Yes, it does." Laurel looked away. "I suspect you know about John Miller and me."

"Yes, ma'am. I just happened to see his car here several times. He's a good man."

"Do good men do what he did---lead you to believe they aren't married?"

"Can't always help who you fall in love with, Miz Mackenzie."

"I suppose not. But why does it happen when there's no possibility of fulfilling the relationship?"

"Maybe you'll understand in time, ma'am. Things aren't always evident right at first."

"One good thing has come from it. I know, firsthand, how Claire felt. That's what had stopped my writing. I hadn't experienced what Claire did."

"And now you have, Ma'am. You been worried about finishing your book, and in your mind you asked for help. You got it. Now you can start writing again."

"You make things sound so simple."

"No ma'am, they aren't. Anytime there's human beings concerned, things can get mighty complicated."

"I have a feeling you could help uncomplicate them, Barney."

The old man's eyes rested on Laurel's face. She could see the tears in them. "I'm trying, ma'am, the best I can."

Barney rose from the rocking chair. "Did you see what's in this room? I'd say we done found ourselves some treasure. All these things must have belonged to the Kilgores."

Laurel had been so intent on the conversation with Barney, she'd failed to notice that the room was filled with an assortment of furniture, paintings, trunks and even a red gown on a dress form. Then she noticed the missing chairs from the dining room suite she'd bought from Barney. She was soon lost in examining the contents of the room. Suddenly, she stopped a few feet from a portrait leaning against the wall in a shadowed corner.

"Dear God in heaven, it's Claire! I know it is."

Laurel looked to Barney, but he had gone. "Where are you? Have you disappeared on me again?"

Not only was he nowhere to be found, but all traces of the mess left by their desire to get into the secret room were gone. Laurel ran to one of the windows at the front of the house and looked out just in time to see his truck turning onto the main road.

The writing came easily for Laurel for a while, but then the inspiration suddenly stopped, and the only thing that would come to her was Barney's words. Don't you worry none, Miss Claire. I'll take care of the baby.

Jane readily accepted Laurel's invitation to lunch. She needed to apologize for the way she had broken the news of John Miller's wife.

"You didn't know what was going on," Laurel assured her as they finished eating. "You really did me a favor, and now I need another one. Would you read the new chapters I've written?"

Jane followed her into the den. "Good, you've been able to resume your writing. Eva said she thought you might. That's why we didn't call you."

"Someone's been trying."

"I expect it was John," Jane said, taking the manuscript. "He's terribly concerned about you."

"It's a little late for that."

"He would like to talk to you."

"I'm not ready to face him yet, Jane."

"Maybe when he gets back?"

"Where is he?"

"I don't know. He just said he'd be gone for about a week."

"Maybe he and his wife are having a second honeymoon."

"Laurel, he doesn't love her."

"You get a divorce if you don't love someone."

"It's his son. He doesn't want to leave him. He so badly wanted a child and when this woman told him she was pregnant, he married her."

"Oh, that's a damned good reason."

"Try to understand, Laurel. John and I and our cousin in Savannah are the only people left in our family. John needed to have a child."

"And what about you, Jane?"

Jane stared at the manuscript. "Some things aren't meant to be," she said.

Laurel sat quietly until Jane read the last chapter. "You know about my baby, don't you, Laurel? Did Eva tell you?"

"No, she didn't."

Then it had to be John. What did he tell you?"

"Just that the child was Lucien's, and it was adopted when you were in Savannah."

"The other day you said you were born in Savannah."

"It's not me, Jane. I'm not your daughter."

"I was hoping."

"I know. I think we should go there. Maybe your cousin will help you find out where your daughter is."

Jane handed the manuscript back to Laurel. "Yes. We'll go, but not just yet. You've written that Claire is pregnant and plans to give the baby away. You want me to tell you what it feels like. Don't you?"

Laurel nodded. "If you want to."

"I haven't even told Eva everything. But maybe it's time I tell someone."

They talked all afternoon, and Laurel shared Jane's grief. It was dark before Jane left and Laurel began writing.

At midnight, she was still at the computer. Claire was close. Laurel felt their spirits join together. She tried to shake it off, but it was too strong.

As the grandfather clock in the hallway struck one, Laurel felt herself rise from the chair, move down the hall and up the stairs. She entered the doorway Barney had made into the walled-up room. She was aware of something in her hand. It was the letter opener from her writing desk. She stopped before the painting. "You cannot be born," the unfamiliar voice escaped her lips. "You must die!" she cried as she plunged the letter opener into Claire's image.

Laurel was aware of being led to Claire's room where she crawled into bed. Someone pulled the covers over her shoulders and whispered in her ear, "Everything gonna be all right, Miss Claire. I'll take care of the baby."

Eva received Laurel's call early the next morning. Within fifteen minutes she was at Belle Rouge. "Thank God you called. I knew something was wrong. What is it?"

Laurel related the details of the night as she took Eva upstairs. "I became Claire," she said."

Eva gasped when she saw the letter opener plunged into the painting. "Her stomach is ripped open!"

"Claire wanted her baby dead," Laurel replied. "I have to know why."

Eva and Laurel spent the rest of the morning at the courthouse going through the records for any clue about what happened to Claire's child.

They were on their way home when Laurel spoke. "Claire couldn't have that much hate for Philippe Dumont's baby," she said. "She had loved him. He did something cruel to her, but she would love his baby. I know she would."

Eva's eyes lit up. "If it were his," she said.

"It wasn't Philippe's! That's it, Eva. The baby belonged to someone else."

"But who?"

"Barney knows the truth. I'm sure of it."

"Where is he Laurel? Take me to him."

"I don't know where Barney lives. He only comes around when I need him for some project."

When Eva did not respond, Laurel said, "I imagined him. Right?"

"Not exactly. He may have some unfinished business here on earth."

"Are you saying he's a ghost?"

"Let's get back to Belle Rouge," Eva suggested.

The warm March days had brought the crimson maples into bud. As they passed under them, Eva asked. "Have you ever wondered why these trees seem to be in perpetual care? Red maples don't have a long life span. Someone must have periodically replaced them."

"I've never thought about it," Laurel replied. "Did Barney do that, too?"

"Maybe. These trees are what caught your eye when you first saw the place. Aren't they? Maybe you've been guided here all along."

"Why?"

"To solve the mystery of Belle Rouge, a mystery strong enough to manifest Barnabas."

"Sumner Kilgore's jockey?"

"You have not connected the two names---Barney and Barnabas?" Eva asked.

"No. When did you?"

"It became obvious when you told me about the jockey. I didn't mention it because I didn't want to scare you."

"Maybe that's why Barney, or Barnabas, doesn't tell me everything at once," Laurel added. "He reveals a little at a time."

"I think you're right. And I believe we all---you, Jane, me and John---know some part of this mystery. Your coming to Cedarville set everything in motion."

"And Barney knows everything."

"You're the one he can get through to, Laurel."

"It was him with me last night. I think he's watching over me."

"Just as he did with Claire, but he can only do so much," Eva warned. "You must be careful. Someone desperately wants to conceal the truth about Belle Rouge."

"Is there a second ghost?" Laurel asked.

"Maybe. But there's something even more frightening. Maybe it's not a ghost we need to fear. Maybe it's someone who's alive and among us now."

## CHAPTER 18

Laurel couldn't believe she'd forgotten about the papers John Miller had given her. She rummaged through the desk and finally found them.

Nothing caught her attention until she came to a page that must have been in Preston Miller's own handwriting. It was a detailed account of the training of Shadow Dancer as well as a description of the Gold Cup race---the one in which Claire had ridden.

Laurel sat down at the computer and began to write:

Alexandra Lennox sat in the parlor of the mansion at Belle Rouge, impatiently tapping her foot. She was not surprised Sumner Kilgore kept her waiting, for she knew he still blamed her for introducing his daughter to Philippe Dumont. Her nervousness mounted as she heard his footsteps in the foyer.

"Well well, back to the scene of the crime?" Sumner jeered. "If you've come to check on Dumont's wife, she's not here. She ran off with one of the field hands."

"Don't play into his hands," Alexandra told herself. "One could never win against Sumner Kilgore by exchanging barbs. Patience would be the only way."

Kilgore eyed the young man seated next to her. "And who is this? Another suitor you've picked for Claire?"

"This is my nephew, Bruce MacCallum," she said, ignoring the jab. "How is Claire?" Alexandra asked.

"She's as well as could be expected. What are you up to?"

"Sit down, Sumner, and quit being so suspicious. I've simply come to make amends with an old friend. I want to apologize to you for being a meddlesome old woman."

Sumner Kilgore roared with laughter. "If that's not a first, Alexandra Lennox apologizing."

"We've been friends too long to let someone like Dumont come between us," she said. "At least you were clever enough to spot his true nature."

Sumner shook his head. "I never thought I'd live to see this day."

"We owe it to Lily to keep our friendship going."

The smile left Sumner Kilgore's face. "Perhaps we do. I'll tell Claire you're here."

When Kilgore disappeared up the staircase, Bruce MacCallum was the first to speak. "Your lip must be bitten through, Aunt Alex. Never would I expect you to humble yourself like that to anyone."

"My lip's bitten clear through. That was the most difficult thing I've ever had to do. I don't usually lie like that. One thing wasn't a lie, though, I do owe this to Lily and to Claire."

The sight of the pale, thin young woman who walked into the room made Alexandra Lennox gasp. She doubted she would have even known her at a distance. Only when Claire saw Alexandra was there any glimmer of light in the eyes of Lily Kilgore's daughter.

"Claire, this is my nephew, Bruce. Come sit down beside us."

"Thank you, but I'll sit over here. My father's gone to the stable. He thought you might want to see his entry for the Gold Cup go through a workout. They'll be ready as soon as he saddles up."

"I really came to see you. How have you been doing?"

"I'm all right, Mrs. Lennox."

Alexandra could not help but notice how Claire watched her nephew with suspicion. "Bruce came to see the horses," she said. "He trains mine in Europe. Why don't you go on ahead of us, Bruce. Sumner would delight in showing you how to train---his way."

Bruce MacCallum gladly took the hint from his aunt. "It was good to meet you, Miss Kilgore."

Alexandra and Claire sat in awkward silence for a few minutes. Finally, Claire spoke in a barely audible voice. "I thought you were mad at me."

"Child, come sit next to me. How could I ever be angry with you?"

Alexandra put her arm around the trembling girl. She could feel Claire's body tense but she did not remove her arm. "There, there, it's all right. Just put your head here on my shoulder."

Claire collapsed into a sob. "I've missed you so," she said.

"And I've missed you. I'm so ashamed of what I did to you."

"It wasn't your fault, Mrs. Lennox. It was mine for being so foolish."

"Please call me Alexandra once again. It will make me believe you have forgiven me."

"There's nothing to forgive. You've been so good to me."

"Doctor James has taken good care of you, hasn't he?"

"Yes. He's very kind. My mother said he would be."

"Did your mother talk often about Timothy?"

"No, but I could see they were good friends. He took Mother's d...death, very hard."

"That's understandable," Alexandra added. "He was probably the first friend Lily made when she came to Kentucky. Now, tell me about yourself. Are you keeping busy?"

"No, I haven't felt like doing much."

"You're not helping Barnabas with any of the horses?"

"He's busy with my father's good horse, Scarlet Satan."

"Do you know what's become of Shadow Dancer?"

"I hear Sheriff Miller's not training the colt," Claire sighed.

Alexandra rose to her feet. "Well, let's go see this horse your father's so high on."

When they approached the saddling area, it was plain to see Sumner Kilgore was highly agitated.

"Dammit, Barnabas! I told you I didn't want to hear anything else about Shadow Dancer. Do you think I would have given that colt to Claire if he were any good? I would have trained him for myself if he were decent. If you'll concentrate on what you're doing, you'll be riding the winner."

"Mornin', Miz Lennox," Barnabas tipped his cap. "Mornin', Miss Claire."

"Get the damn horse on the track, Barnabas!"

"Yes sir, Mr. Kilgore. I'll work her a mile and a half today. We'll see what she can do."

With pleasure, Alexandra Lennox had seen the anger flash in Claire's eyes. Good girl, she said to herself. Let that anger simmer and you'll find the courage to do what I'm going to ask of you. Together we will deal Sumner Kilgore a blow from which he'll never recover.

"That's a fine looking animal, sir," Bruce MacCallum said.

"Bet you don't have anything like her in Europe," Sumner gloated.

"No indeed, we don't. We don't value speed as much as we do stamina."

"It takes both stamina and speed to win here, Mr. MacCallum. Good God! Look at that mare cover ground. No horse will be able to run with her."

"Sumner!" Alexandra averted his attention when she saw her nephew pull out his pocket watch. "Come here and tell me the breeding of your mare."

A big smile crossed Kilgore's face. "She's not for sale."

"I know. You'd be foolish to get rid of such a good horse. Would she happen to be related to Red Satan?"

"She's the only horse I have left that's by him."

"She doesn't have Satan's spirit," Claire added.

"I'd say we're all the more fortunate for that," Sumner replied.

"The will to win is more important than anything, Father."

"Breeding and conformation are what makes a winner, daughter. Besides, when did you get to be such an expert, Claire? Oh, I remember. It's when you taught that white-legged runt, Shadow Dancer, to lead. Wasn't it? That's what made you a trainer."

Bruce MacCallum replaced his pocket watch as Barnabas crossed the finish line with Scarlet Satan. "You have a very nice horse, Mr. Kilgore. No doubt she'll be the favorite for the Gold Cup."

"No doubt at all. If you're still around the last of July, Mr. MacCallum, you'd be wise to put some money on her."

"I'll be here, sir. Thought I might learn some new tricks from you Americans."

"That's a bright nephew you have there, Alexandra. Maybe you'll bring him again soon. I'll be happy to show him a few things," Kilgore beamed.

"That's hospitable of you, Sumner. Of course Bruce will come again," she smiled. "I suppose we'll visit a bit longer with Claire. Would you mind if Claire showed Bruce and me some of the farms in the area? We'll scout out your competition."

"Most of the locals are scared off," Kilgore laughed. "But sure, go ahead. It'll do Claire good to get out. All she wants is to stay in her room. I was afraid she'd start to go up in that observatory just like her mother did. Yes, go ahead, take her. Get her mind on something besides herself."

Alexandra noticed that Claire's step quickened as they walked toward the house. Her eyes were intense, and her jaw was set.

"Why does my father talk as if I weren't even present," she muttered. "And he's wrong. I know he is. Shadow is a runner. He's small, and he does have those white legs my father hates. But he has heart, Alexandra. His heart would make him a winner."

Alexandra Lennox put her arm around Claire. "Sometimes it's heart that carries us through anything," she said. "Now, let's go for a ride. Bruce and I want to make you a business offer. But first, we'll need to pick up another passenger."

The carriage stopped for Dr. James. When they were on their way again, Claire spoke.

"Something's going on. Are any of you going to let me in on it?"

"We're on our way to Preston Miller's farm," Alexandra smiled. "I think you'll see something that will please you very much."

The excitement in Claire's eyes was evident. "Sheriff Miller's going to race Shadow, isn't he? Mr. MacCallum, you're doing the training?"

"Yes, I am. And I think you're right about the horse. He has a fine heart."

"Can he beat Scarlet Satan? My father's horse has so much speed."

"Your father's horse has speed for a little over a mile. The last quarter was terribly slow. He's going to try to steal the race--get so far ahead that no horse can catch her. Our task is to train Shadow to keep in striking distance and have enough left to sprint that last quarter faster than Scarlet Satan."

"That's a lot to ask of any animal," Claire sighed.

"Indeed it is, but I think we have the one horse that can do it," Bruce MacCallum assured her.

The carriage pulled through the entryway of the Miller farm and continued toward the back of the property, where it came to a stop at the edge of a line of trees. The passengers got out and walked two hundred yards into the woods. A training area had been built there, not in the usual oval shape, but in a straight line of about a quarter mile. Preston Miller waited for them with several of his hired hands.

"Hello," Miller called. "I see you've brought her with you."

Claire reached for the burly man's hand. "I'm so pleased you're going to enter Shadow in the Gold Cup. I just pray he has a chance to win."

"There's a chance. Mr. MacCallum's doing a fine job."

Bruce MacCallum gave the exercise boy a leg up. "Work him at a slow gallop for three miles," he instructed.

Back and forth on the quarter-mile path the workout continued. Each time at the end of the path the rider would alternate the direction of the horse's turn.

Claire inched her way forward until she stood at Bruce MacCallum's side. "I've never seen training like this," she said.

"It's the European way," he answered. "It builds stamina."

"Here in America we train on the oval, and stress is continually on the left side of the animal. You train on a straight line so there's equal stress."

"You're very bright, Miss Kilgore," MacCallum smiled.

"How do you keep a horse from drifting out on the turns when he's in a race?" Claire asked.

"That will come, but not until this part of the training is finished."

When Shadow Dancer completed the three miles, Bruce MacCallum called to the rider. "All right, you know what to do."

The exercise boy turned the animal and rapped it on its flank with the whip. Shadow lunged forward with an unbelievable burst of speed.

At the end of the quarter mile, MacCallum called. "That's enough. Rub him down and cool him out."

Claire was silent until they reached the others. "I think Shadow can beat Scarlet Satan, but not without a good jockey. It's too bad Barnabas can't ride for us."

"It's a pity," Alexandra agreed. "A good rider is all we lack. Is there anyone at Belle Rouge Barnabas has trained?"

"No one. Only...."

"Only you, Claire," Alexandra interrupted. "There's only one person who could bring Shadow Dancer home a winner---and that's you."

"Alexandra, my father would die! Why he's only just started to let me attend the races. He's not even sure that's proper. If I rode in a race, he would literally die."

"Are you afraid to ride?" Bruce MacCallum asked.

"No, I'm not afraid!" Claire shot back at him. "I can ride any horse."

"As well as Barnabas?"

"Mr. MacCallum, Barney says I have better hands than he does."

"If you don't want to ride, we'll let the exercise boy do it. We have to race. Shadow deserves a go at it, just like you told your father. I'll tell the boy he's going to ride."

"No wait. I would like to ride, but my father would never allow it."

"He doesn't have to know," Alexandra winked.

"How can you keep something like that a secret?"

"I'm going to tell Sumner that I want you to accompany me while I show Bruce some of our country. The trip should take about a month and a half. We should be back just in time for the Gold Cup. Doctor James is once again going to agree that a trip would do you good. Sumner will say yes."

"But I still don't see..."

"The three of you will stay here at my farm," Sheriff Miller interjected.

"Do you really think it will work?" Claire asked.

"I know it will," Alexandra replied.

With little protest, Sumner agreed that the trip with Alexandra should take place. His only admonition was that they should return in time to see Scarlet Satan win the Gold Cup.

The days of intense training continued. Shadow Dancer seemed to thrive on his workouts. His well-developed muscles rippled under his shining black coat, and his eyes and ears remained alert. His intelligence coupled with his willingness to run pleased all who worked with him.

Bruce MacCallum paid close attention to the animal's legs. He would check them for any signs of heat. Periodically he packed them in the clay mud that abounded on the Miller farm.

Claire, too, was eager to learn. Barnabas had given her a good foundation in riding, but Bruce MacCallum refined her style. "Ride low in the saddle, less wind resistance," he would call to her.

He agreed with Barnabas' appraisal of her hands. The feel she had for a horse's mouth was incredible. He also noticed she could anticipate the animal's moves. He had never seen a rider so attuned to a horse.

Alexandra busied herself sewing a riding suit for Claire. The shirt was pure white silk with rows of blue diamonds spaced evenly on it. Claire and Shadow will certainly be easy to spot in the race, she had laughingly told her cohorts.

Doctor James made periodic stops at the farm. He had not seen Claire so radiant in years. But he had several concerns. He felt there was no way they could keep Claire's identity a secret if she won the race. And he hoped Alexandra was really orchestrating this to benefit Claire. He wondered if it had more to do with her dislike for Sumner Kilgore than it did with her concern for his daughter.

"Laurel? Laurel!" she heard her name. "Can you give me a hand?" Eva was trying to make her way through the front door, two suitcases in her hand.

"What are you doing?"

"What does it look like?" Eva grinned. "I'm moving in for a while."

"I'm happy to have your company. But why?"

"Too many things are going on. It's getting more dangerous with that slashing of Claire's painting. You need someone here while John's gone."

"John's not going to come here when he gets back."

"I don't mean HERE in the house, Laurel. I mean here in town to keep a close eye on the farm and Lucien Caulder."

Laurel took one of the suitcases and put it in the guest room on the first floor. "Here you are, the room next to mine."

"And I'm going to make sure you stay in it with none of this sleeping in Claire's room," Eva insisted.

"Claire's not in danger now. She's getting ready to ride Shadow Dancer in the Cup Race. Do you want to read the chapter?"

"You bet I do," Eva replied.

When she finished reading, she handed it back to Laurel. "I do believe that's some of the best writing you've ever done. I can see how you'd have empathy for Claire, with your both loving horses as you do."

"You're speaking of her as if she were alive, Eva."

"Yes, I know. It feel's as if she's here in the house."

# CHAPTER 19

With Eva's encouragement, Laurel's writing continued at a rapid pace.

Sumner Kilgore's father had donated the land for the Cedarville track in the early 1800's. The lay of the land was unusual. The course had been dug out just below the crest and around the hill. The spectators could see the entire race when seated near the clubhouse atop the rise.

The day of the race dawned unusually cool and cloudy for late July. Overnight rains had left the track with puddles of standing water.

"Don't worry," Bruce MacCallum assured them. "These conditions will favor our entry."

The plan was for MacCallum, Sheriff Miller and Shadow Dancer to arrive early so the horse would have time to settle in. Alexandra and Claire would arrive just before post time so no one would recognize the jockey listed simply as 'le Claire'.

MaCallum and Miller were saddling Shadow when Sumner Kilgore approached.

"So, MacCallum, this is the real reason you're here in the states," he laughed. "Preston, you've wasted the money you're paying him. You don't have a prayer."

"Bruce thinks we have a chance. After all, second place pays pretty well."

"Second place is all you can hope for, Sheriff," Kilgore sneered.

Sumner quickly headed for Barnabas and Scarlet Satan.

"He's worried," the sheriff whispered. "He may try some kind of a trick in the race. Do you think Claire's up to it?"

"I'm going to tell her to stay on the outside and away from Scarlet Satan," the trainer answered.

"Here they come," Preston Miller said excitedly.

Alexandra whisked Claire to the saddling ring, then hurried to a vantage point by the clubhouse.

"Claire, we'll do just as we planned," Bruce MacCallum instructed. "Let Barnabas have the lead. He's certain to hug the rail and save ground so his horse will have something left for the final quarter. Stay behind him, but well off the rail. The footing is a little more firm there. When you make your move at the quarter pole, don't let Barnabas draw you to the inside. He'll come over on you and cut you off if you do. Stay to the outside, whatever you do."

"Riders up," came the call.

MacCallum gave his rider a leg up. "Keep that cap pulled down, and no one will recognize you. Remember, stay to the outside."

Five horses answered the call to the post. Scarlet Satan had drawn the first position, the Tennessee mare the second, followed by the bay from Virginia, Shadow Dancer and finally the gelding from Lexington on the outside.

The start was clean, and Scarlet Satan soon opened up a two-length lead with, Claire on Shadow content to follow MacCallum's instructions. Unexpectedly, the pesky gelding hung just to the outside of Claire's horse.

Bruce MacCallum placed himself halfway between the quarter pole and the finish. The sheriff joined Alexandra on the hill.

"Has she got a chance?" Alexandra asked.

“The race isn’t going quite like we anticipated,” Miller answered. “We didn’t think the gelding would be so close. Bruce told Claire to pass Scarlet Satan on the outside. She may not be able to if the gelding doesn’t fold.

For a mile, the positions of the horses did not change, but the three front runners widened their lead. The Tennessee mare and the Virginia bay were clearly outdistanced.

At the three quarters, Barnabas drew his riding crop from under his arm but only waved it at Scarlet Satan. The mare quickly moved out to a three-length lead.

“Not yet, Claire,” MacCallum said under his breath. “Let Scarlet Satan come back to you. Barnabas knows his horse is going to tire.” Suddenly MacCallum slammed his fist against the fence. “Damn that gelding! He’s hanging in. Claire’s going to be trapped if she’s not careful.”

As they turned for home, Barnabas hit Scarlet Satan with two quick taps. He could feel no response. The hoofbeats behind him were gaining. He began to doubt his horse’s ability to hold on. The muddy track was taking its toll.

He glanced over his shoulder. Shadow Dancer had closed to within one length. The Lexington gelding was just a half length to the outside. He could tell the gelding was driving, but Sheriff Miller’s horse was steady and resolute.

Barnabas was about to gamble that Shadow’s rider was green. He eased Scarlet Satan out from the rail just enough to impede his rival.

Claire pulled her horse back to keep from clipping the heel of Barnabas’ mount. The gelding quickly closed the gap, and Shadow Dancer had nowhere to go but to the rail.

Shadow saw the hole open up just as Claire did, and he dove for it. But Barnabas moved over. Again Claire pulled Shadow up.

When they passed the eighth pole, Scarlet Satan was a length ahead of the gelding, and Shadow Dancer was trapped behind them in third.

Claire could tell the pace was beginning to slow. Her horse was full of run, but he had no place to go. Suddenly, the tiring Scarlet Satan bumped the rail leaving a small space between her and the gelding. Shadow inched his way between them.

Claire felt her boots rub against the boots of the other two riders. The quarters were too tight for her to use the whip, so she loosened Shadow's reins.

"Go boy!" she cried. "Go! Go!"

At the sound of the voice, Barnabas turned his head. He got a good look at the face of the jockey on the white-legged horse. He knew Scarlet Satan was finished, so he put his whip away. The gelding, too, was falling back.

Shadow Dancer was two lengths to the clear when they crossed the finish line. And the gelding was one length ahead of the Kilgore entry.

Claire quickly headed her horse back to where Bruce MacCallum was waiting.

"Alexandra's waiting for you just over the fence," he told her.

She hopped down and was over the fence before Scarlet Satan returned to Sumner Kilgore. As she got in the buggy, she saw her father pull Barnabas from the saddle.

"You son of a bitch," his voice rang above the crowd. "You never even used your whip." Kilgore grabbed the crop and unmercifully lashed the black man.

"Claire! Get back in this buggy!" Alexandra called. "You'll only make matters worse for Barnabas."

"I think Barnabas recognized me when I passed him."

"He won't tell Sumner. Come on. We have to get out of here."

Sheriff Miller grabbed Sumner by the collar. "My God, man. Let him be. Your horse was finished. Why should Barnabas whip the animal?"

"Stay out of this!" Kilgore yelled.

Preston pushed him away from Barnabas and Bruce MacCallum helped the bleeding jockey up off the ground.

"You nigger-loving bastard!" Sumner called to him. "Why don't you take him back to England with you. He's no good to me anymore."

MacCallum handed Barnabas his handkerchief. "That's a nasty looking cut on your cheek. Better let Doctor James have a look at it."

"No. I can't do that," Barnabas protested. "Doctor James'll be in trouble if he treats a black man."

"Dear God, I don't understand the rationale of these Americans," MacCallum shook his head. "Why should it matter what color a man's skin is if he needs help?"

"I don't need no doctor, sir. I'll take care of it myself."

"What about Kilgore? Do you dare go back to Belle Rouge?"

"I don't think Mr. Kilgore will be home anytime soon, sir. I'd say he'll keep company with a bottle at the saloon for a day or two. After he sleeps it off, he'll cool down."

"You don't have to put up with him. Do come back to England with me. I could use your help on the farm."

"I think I be needed here, sir. Miss Claire's only got me to look out for her now. And don't worry none, I'll never tell Mr. Kilgore who your rider was. She was damned good! Wasn't she, sir?"

"Indeed she was, Barnabas."

"If you don't mind me being a little bold, Mr. MacCallum, I believe you a little sweet on Miss Claire."

"Is it that noticeable?" Bruce MacCallum blushed.

"Deed it is to me, sir. Maybe she's the one who should go to England with you."

"If I thought there was even a chance, I'd ask her. But I can't seem to make any headway with her. Every time I start to say something personal to her, she changes the subject. All she'll talk about is horses. I'm not even sure she likes me. Is she this cold to every man, or is it just me?"

"She's been hurt bad, sir. I don't know if any man will ever get close to her again."

"If Sumner Kilgore's the only example she's got, no wonder she's the way she is," Bruce MacCallum replied.

That night, Genevieve hitched a horse to the buggy. She checked the bottle under the seat to make sure it would not tip over. She patted her pocket. The matches were there.

The buggy moved slowly and quietly beside the mansion. She knew Barnabas was asleep on a pallet in the kitchen, for he would not leave Claire alone in the house. Genevieve glanced up toward the second floor. Claire's room was dark.

"I'll take care of you too, Missy. I'll be the one sleeping in that house real soon."

When Laurel finished reading the chapter out loud, Eva said, "That's when Genevieve burned Dr. James' house down. I think you may have solved one part of the mystery. I agree it was Genevieve who killed him."

Laurel put the manuscript into the file cabinet. Then she asked, "If Barnabas can manifest himself to me, can Genevieve do the same?"

"It's possible," Eva replied. "Do you think you've seen her?"

"Could she have been 'Nila' on the plane or the woman at Keeneland who spotted my colt's ankle?"

"I doubt it, Laurel. That woman wants to help. I know Genevieve wouldn't do that. Some things are more akin to Genevieve: something spooked your mare and made her jump the graveyard fence. Then there's Jane. Could Genevieve have pushed her down the stairs?"

"She was pushed?" Laurel frowned.

"She thinks she was," Eva said. "I'm sure Genevieve pushed Lily from the glass room. Doctor James thought so too, and maybe he had proof. That's why Genevieve had to get rid of him."

"If you're right, and I think you are, why is she after Jane?"

"When we know that, we'll have solved another part of the mystery."

John Miller left the Office of Vital Statistics at the state capitol. He held a folder, thick with papers. He got in his car, reached for the mobile phone and dialed Jane's number.

"Jane, how are you? ---- I'm in Frankfort, doing a little investigating, on a couple of matters. ----- Is Laurel all right? ---- I know she's hurt and I'd like a chance to apologize. OK, I'll give her some time. ------ Do you know if she's read Preston Miller's papers yet? ----- Good! I'm happy Eva's with her. Listen, I want to tell you something. I didn't give Laurel everything Preston had. I kept something very interesting. ----- It has to do with Lucien. ------ Just try to keep Laurel away from him. Have somebody stay with her all the time. It's very important. I've got to go now. I'll see you in a few days. Bye."

John didn't want to share his other suspicions with Jane. Instead, he sent a telegram to a sheriff he knew in Beaufort,

South Carolina. He was sure his friend would help him locate Jane's daughter. He placed his findings in his briefcase along side another paper. It was a report from a blood test. The boy was not his son.

As soon as Jane hung up, she went to Belle Rouge, and related what John had told her.

"I don't intend to be kept a prisoner," Laurel said.

"You'll not be a prisoner. You'll have a couple of shadows," Jane grinned. "We'll be your bodyguards."

Eva didn't smile. "I think we need to do some private eye work, too. Didn't John tell you anything he found out about Lucien?"

"No. He just said that he'd be back in a few days. He said he was looking into a COUPLE of things, but he didn't say what they were."

"Well, what's the next step?" Laurel asked.

"You get to writing", Eva said. "I want to know if Sumner found out who rode Shadow Dancer."

"We all talk as if I'm writing facts. All this is just something that's coming out of my imagination."

"But my guess is, you're right on the mark. Now, Jane, if you'll stay here with Laurel and keep her nose to the grindstone, I'm going upstairs to take a closer look at what's in the secret room. Maybe I can pick up some 'feelings' when I'm around the Kilgores' things."

"All right, Miss Mackenzie," Jane teased. "You start writing."

Laurel rested her eyes for a moment and began.

Claire awoke with a start. No remembrance of a nightmare lingered with her, but her fear was real. Then she saw it. A red glow flickered across the wall. She threw back the covers and ran toward the window. Something was on fire at the Junction.

She dressed hastily and ran down the stairs. Barnabas wasn't in the kitchen. When she found him at the barn, he'd already saddled a horse.

"Give me a hand up," she demanded. "I'm going with you."

Claire clung to Barnabas' waist as the horse galloped down the drive and onto the main road.

"Can you see what's burning?" she asked.

"Not sure, Miss Claire. I'll be able to tell soon."

Barnabas stopped the horse on a rise to give it a breather. "Oh no!" he cried.

Claire peered over his shoulder. "What is it?"

He spurred the horse. "It's Doctor James' house!"

Sheriff Miller pushed his way through the crowd until he found the station master. "Did any of them get out?" he asked.

"Mrs. James and the boys left yesterday morning for Virginia, but the Doctor..." his voice broke. "But Doctor James is in there. He came home right after the Gold Cup. Said he was tired and was going to bed early. We tried to rescue him, but the flames were too intense."

"Did you see anybody hanging around here?" the sheriff asked.

"Well..." the station master hesitated.

"Go on man. Did you see anybody?"

"Several people saw Mr. Kilgore's Barnabas coming out the back door of Doc's house just about sundown. He had a bandage on his face."

Sheriff Miller stared into the fire. "There's no way this was an accident. It spread too fast."

The approaching hoofbeats caught his attention. "Barnabas! Come here," he called. "Why did you bring Claire?"

"She wouldn't stay home, sir. I had to."

"Were you here this afternoon?"

Barnabus hung his head. "Yes sir, I was. "Doctor James said everything would be all right if he treated my cuts. But he was wrong. He was wrong."

"Go back to Belle Rouge. Get Claire out of here."

A loud voice came from the crowd. "Looks like the two jockeys are still in cahoots."

"Sumner, go home. You're drunk," the sheriff commanded.

"You Miller, Alexandra, Barney and my own daughter---you all plotted against me," Kilgore accused.

The Sheriff tightened his fist. "Shut up, you idiot. One of your best friends died in that inferno and all you can talk about is a damned horse race."

"A good friend?" Sumner laughed. "A good friend to my wife, maybe."

Miller's blow caught Kilgore squarely on the jaw, and his knees buckled. "Somebody get him out of here!"

Barnabas and a couple of bystanders dragged the limp body to the buggy where Genevieve was waiting.

Her eyes narrowed when she spotted Barnabas. "Get away," she commanded. "I'll take care of Mister Sumner."

Barnabas watched the buggy disappear into the darkness. He fell to his knees and buried his head in his hands.

"What have I done?" he moaned. "Why did I let him treat me? That's why his house was set on fire."

A picture flashed in his mind. Just a few hours earlier, Genevieve's naked body lay against his, her hand soothing his aching muscles. Slowly she crawled on top of him. Her words were warm against his ear.

"You know who Shadow's jockey was don't you? Are you gonna tell?"

"I promised Miss Claire I wouldn't," he said. "She tricked me. That's how Mr. Sumner found out. Gen told him and now, because of me, Miss Claire will have to suffer."

Barnabas got up and went to Claire. She was staring into the fire. "We gotta go," he said.

They rode quietly until they turned into the drive of Belle Rouge. Then Barnabas broke the silence. "Your father knows you rode in the race today. He's gonna be awful mad when he sobers up. It's not gonna be safe here for either of us. Mr. MacCallum asked me to come and work for him in England. He wants you to come too."

"Belle Rouge is my home, Barnabas."

"Miz Lennox is goin'. They bought Shadow Dancer from Sheriff Miller. They gonna race him over there. Miss Claire, they're leaving day after tomorrow. Please come with us."

"I can't. My father needs me."

For the rest of the night, Claire lay in bed, staring at the wall, unable to close her eyes. She watched until the red glow on the wall was absorbed by the sunrise. As she lay there she heard what she knew to be Barnabas' footsteps on the gravel outside her window. He'd board the morning train to Louisville to keep his rendezvous with Alexandra and Bruce.

She could not blame him for leaving. It was too dangerous for him at Belle Rouge. She wished it were not so. First Ross, then her mother, Doctor James and now Barnabas. They were all gone, but she would not leave Sumner Kilgore, too.

There were no signs of Genevieve or Sumner during the day, but just at nightfall, she heard him.

"Lily...Lily," the pitiful cry came. "Lily, where are you?"

Claire opened the kitchen door and watched as her father staggered up the walk from the stable. She hurried to his side, and he put his arm on her shoulder.

"Lean on me. I'll help you," she said.

"Everybody's betrayed me," he cried. "You love me, don't you, Lily?"

Claire put her arm around her father's waist to steady him. "Watch your step. Come sit down at the table, and I'll fix you something to eat."

Sumner plopped down in a chair, but when Claire moved toward the stove, he grabbed her arm.

"I knew you couldn't stay away from me too long, Lily. I knew you'd love me again."

"Let go, you're hurting me," Claire said.

"No, Lily, don't do this. Don't pull away from me again."

"Stop it!" she demanded.

"I've been patient with you long enough, woman. You'll not deny me another time."

Claire struggled to free herself, but he was too strong. She tried to scream, but his foul-smelling mouth was hard against hers. His hand was tearing at her clothing while he forced her onto the table. She could feel him groping at her, forcing her legs apart.

When she awoke, she was in her room. She tried to turn over, but the pain forced her back. Someone placed a cup to her lips. For a second she remembered the horror, but then a soothing liquid balm spread over her and she fell asleep again.

When she awoke the second time, someone was standing over her. The voice echoed from a faraway place, but she could make out the words.

"Oh, dear lord. What have they done to you?"

She reached out and the black hand enclosed hers. "Barnabas, you've come back," she whispered.

Each of the passing days slipped by meaninglessly, one into the other. Food was unpalatable, left untouched. The bitter tea

Genevieve offered gave Claire blessed relief from the realization of her conscious mind. Remembrances, thoughts, all were obliterated in a surreal world of nothingness.

One day, she became aware of a figure beside her bed. She blinked. She didn't recognize the bearded man with the hollow dark eyes.

"Daughter, you have to eat."

"Father? What's wrong?"

"You've had us worried, Claire. You've been very ill for quite some time."

"What happened?"

"We think you fell the night the fire killed Doctor James."

"Oh, I remember the fire," she said. "It was terrible."

"Do you remember anything else?" Sumner asked.

"No. Nothing after the fire."

"Genevieve's fixed you a tray. Please eat."

"Yes sir, I will. But how long have I been sick?"

"You've been in some sort of a stupor for weeks, but Genevieve's been doctoring you, and now you're better. Eat, then rest."

"Father, where's Barnabas?"

"Breaking a two-year-old colt. I think we have ourselves another Red Satan." Sumner Kilgore paused in the doorway, a slight smile on his face. "You're going to want to be up and about soon to watch him work. He'll win the Gold Cup next year."

When her father left the room, Claire reached under her pillow. Her diary was not there. She slid to the edge of the bed hoping to find the book in the night stand. Carefully, she eased herself into a sitting position. Then it hit her, an unmerciful wave of nausea.

She groaned and fell back against the pillow. Maybe my father's right, she thought. I have to eat something to get my strength back. She forced some of the food down.

Momentarily, she felt a bit better and once again sat up. She searched in the night stand for her diary, but it was not to be found.

"Where could I have left it?" she asked herself. Her hand drew out another book whose pages were blank. "I must write. I'll start a new diary," Claire said.

Laurel stared at the computer screen. "Eva," she cried. "Come downstairs, quickly!"

"What is it?" Jane asked.

When Eva came into the room, Laurel said, "I think Claire had a second diary."

"I know," Eva replied. "Here it is. I found it in the secret room."

Eagerly, Laurel took the book and scanned the first few entries. "You're right, Eva. I am on the mark."

"Please," Jane said, "read it out loud."

"From what I see, Claire has lost track of time. The first entry is dated August or early September.

*My father tells me I have been bedridden for over a month. I have no recollection of that time, except for a few episodes of consciousness. I remember drinking Genevieve's tea. I remember Barnabas came back. When I woke up this time, my father was here in the room. I cannot believe his appearance. He is unshaven and gaunt. But what should I expect of him? He has lost everyone dear to him. And when I betrayed him, it must have been the final blow. I knew how much the race meant to him. Why did I help him go down in defeat? How will I ever make it up to him?*

*I cannot find my diary. I last remember writing in it just before I went with Alexandra and Bruce to stay at Sheriff Miller's for Shadow Dancer's training. I suppose I will find it, but till then I will continue in this new book.*

*I hardly know where to start, except to say that all of us banded together to see to it that Shadow Dancer, not my father's entry, would win the Gold Cup.*

*How humiliating it must have been for my father when he found out I was riding Dancer. Barnabas too, recognized me. I will always wonder if he let me win the race.*

*I went home to Belle Rouge following the race, but I was awakened in the early morning hours. The wall in my room was red with the glow of a fire in the distance. Doctor James' house was burning, and he was inside. The sheriff believes someone set it because the doctor treated Barnabas for the cuts inflicted after the race. I am to blame for this terrible ordeal.*

Laurel closed the book. "That's the only entry Claire made. I think she was drugged too heavily to continue. I'm going to write some more now. I think I know what happened next."

Claire placed the new diary in the night stand. She was surprised at how much better she felt. Did she dare try to stand, she wondered. Shakily she arose, but the nausea struck again. She felt her knees give way, and the blackness came. When she came to, she was in her bed. There were two people arguing in the corner of her room.

"Why didn't you keep a closer eye on her?" Sumner Kilgore growled.

"I can't stay with her every minute," Genevieve said. "Maybe if you got me a servant to do the kitchen work, I could sit with your daughter."

"Get you a servant?" Sumner laughed. "Who the hell do you think you are?"

"You know who I am," Genevieve shot back. "I'm the woman you sleep with. The woman you've always come to even before your wife...."

Laurel turned away from the computer to find that both Jane and Eva had not moved from their chairs. "That's all," she said. "It's as if the door to my imagination has been shut. What do we do now?"

Eva picked up the diary she had just found. "Perhaps if you put yourself in Claire's place and actually wrote as if you were her."

Laurel took the diary from her. She began by scribbling a date on the top of the page. The pencil began to move.

*March 3*

*My mind is so filled with thoughts, but I have been unable to do anything or to write anything for months. My anger and my anguish are overwhelming, and I cannot remember why. It is as if my memory has been erased.*

*I can only hear two voices inside me arguing. No, arguing is not the correct word. One voice chastises while the other whimpers from its refuge in a dark corner, and I don't know why.*

*I seem to be moving about in the physical world as an apparition, unnoticed, invisible.*

*March 5*

*I do not have the energy to get out of bed. The new servant woman has been very attentive. She brought a feather pillow Genevieve made especially for me.*

*March 25*

*I have no sense of purpose, but I feel as if there is something that has taken hold of me...steadily moving me. Sometimes when I am whimpering in that corner of my mind, I think I see a beast forming inside of me. I shake with fear, for I believe I know its purpose. The beast is growing stronger, and I know its name.*

*April 2*

*How comforting it is to be enclosed in the glass room. The spring rain softly sings its lullaby as it closes me off from the view of the inhabitants of Belle Rouge. I see them moving about below me. They have become faceless figures with no names.*

*April...your face is that of Dresden china, so delicate, so fragile, so easily broken. But I, from my high perch, I know what is to become of you. Your tender colors will soon be baked in the heat of July. April, don't you know the beast is sucking the very breath out of you?*

*April 10*

*I cannot go to the glass room today. I must not let myself go there. I must hold on to reality. I have to put their faces back on them. Barnabas, help me. Genevieve sometimes sits and watches me. What does she see---the One or the Two of me? Barnabas...Barnabas...*

*April 20*

*I slept after Genevieve gave me the drink, but even her drugs could not make my mind rest. I felt the beast move.*

*April 24*

*It is two a.m., and I have been unable to rest. Whenever I close my eyes, I dream---or perhaps I'm hallucinating. Yesterday, when Barney took me for a ride, I felt almost like my old self. But the moment I'm in my room and quiet, the strange feelings come back. I try hard to block out the beast, but it grows inside me. Sometimes I think it is trying to devour me.*

*April 28*

*The pain is almost unbearable. I know the beast within me is trying to manifest itself. I must get up. I must find Barnabas.*

When she finished, Laurel read the portion she had just written in the diary.

Jane posed a question. "Do you believe Claire was pregnant with her own father's child?"

"Yes, and I can only imagine what happened next."

"That's exactly what you have to do," Eva said. "We have no other way of knowing."

Laurel stood up. "This is crazy. I write about Claire's second diary and Eva comes in with it in her hand. I pick up a pencil to write in the diary, and I don't feel like it's me who's doing it. I think it's Claire."

"Don't fight your fear," Eva exclaimed. "Write your way through it. For some reason the missing parts of whatever went on here at Belle Rouge are coming through you. You have to go on."

"I'm not sure," Jane said. "Maybe it's John who's found the missing parts."

"Laurel knows what goes on with Claire," Eva said. "John has something else."

"How many more parts are there? We've solved several."

"There's more, Laurel, and I know it. Please write," Eva pleaded.

Once again Laurel turned to the computer:

Claire dragged herself from her bed. By holding onto the wall to steady herself, she managed to make her way to the kitchen. She could hear Genevieve's voice.

"Her time's almost here. You know what has to be done."

"I'm not going to let you kill my own child," Sumner's voice replied.

"Can you bring that kind of a child into this world?"

Kilgore's voice was hardly audible. "No, I can't. Do what you will with the baby."

"What baby?" Claire's voice came from the doorway.

What are you doing out of bed? Get back upstairs!" Genevieve demanded.

"My God, what have I done to you?" Sumner cried.

"Get away from me," Claire pushed his outstretched arms. "Don't touch me. The beast is coming!" she screamed.

Sumner Kilgore leaned against the stones of the blazing fireplace, sobbing uncontrollably.

"Kill the beast," Claire pleaded. "Kill it."

Genevieve's face contorted in the glow of the fire. "I will, just like he did my baby."

"No, Gen, no," came another voice. "No one killed your baby. I took him. He's alive."

"You're lying, Barnabas," Genevieve seethed. "His grave is there in the back field."

"There's no one buried in that grave. Your child is alive. I know where he is. I'll take you to him."

"I have the heir to Belle Rouge?" Genevieve questioned.

Sumner Kilgore wheeled around. "You think I'd give anything to you or your child, you black witch?"

"You got no choice. My boy is your child. He is the rightful heir to Belle Rouge."

"Claire is carrying the heir to my fortune," Sumner yelled.

"No!" Genevieve shouted. "Her baby has to be killed!" Her hand reached for the rifle standing in the corner. She raised it waist high and pointed it at Claire. "It has to die," she cried.

Sumner Kilgore leapt in front of Claire just as Genevieve pulled the trigger. The bullet struck him in the midsection.

Barnabas rushed to him and eased him to the floor. "Mr. Kilgore! It ain't like what she says. It ain't. Miss Claire's baby will be fine. You're not Miss Claire's father. Doctor James was. Miz Lily told me so."

The rifle fell from Genevieve's grip, and she stood, eyes glazed, body reeling. "Doctor James is dead. He don't matter no more. The fire killed him."

"You set that fire?" Barnabas questioned.

Genevieve nodded. "He figured out everything. He was gonna tell Mr. Sumner. I couldn't let that happen."

"Barnabas, stop her," Sumner whispered. "Don't let her hurt Claire."

Claire stared down at Sumner Kilgore then began to inch her way toward Genevieve. "You killed my mother, too," she said. "I remember now. I saw you standing behind her in the glass room. You pushed her."

"I was the one who belonged with Mr. Sumner. She was keeping me from him. She had to die."

"And my brother? How did you kill him?"

Genevieve smiled. "I put a piece of metal in his riding crop."

Sumner Kilgore clutched at Barney's shirt. "Was Timothy really Claire's father?" he asked.

"Yes sir. An' Miss Claire is carrying your child. Ain't nothing gonna be wrong with the baby, sir. Nothing."

A hideous laugh came from Genevieve's throat. "Yes, there will be. I put a spell on Miss Claire, and it will carry through to her baby. Every generation descending from her will suffer from the curse. It will escape none of her heirs who try to own Belle Rouge."

"No!" Barnabas reached out for Claire, but it was too late. With one mighty shove, Claire gave Genevieve a push and she fell backward into the fireplace. Genevieve struggled to her feet. The human column of fire reeled about the room. The curtains ignited. The fire spread quickly.

"Get out," Sumner's feeble voice murmured. "Barnabas, save Claire and the baby."

Barnabas guided Claire toward the door. "Run Missy, run to the barn."

"Come with me, Barnabas," she pleaded.

"No, I can't. I got to stay. I got to save Belle Rouge for you."

# CHAPTER 20

It was after dark when John Miller turned off the interstate and headed into Cedarville. The closer he came, the more he felt the presence of danger. Though he wanted to see Laurel, he knew she wouldn't welcome him. Maybe he should talk to Jane first.

As he came to the road leading to Lucien Caulder's house, for some unexplained reason, he turned. Caulder was pulling out of his driveway as he passed. John turned around and followed the car until it headed south out of Cedarville. He didn't follow his instinct. Instead, he went on to Jane's house. Eva opened the door.

"What are you doing here?" he asked. "I thought you were with Laurel."

"Jane wasn't feeling very well, and Laurel assured me she'd be all right. So I came here."

Suddenly John's thoughts came together. He knew why Lucien Caulder was heading out of Cedarville. "Call the sheriff's office and tell them I need backup. Tell them to meet me at Belle Rouge on the double."

"What is it, John?" Eva called after him.

"Get on the damned phone and do what I told you!" he yelled. "Now! Do it now!"

Miller's car spun out of the driveway and sped down the street. He had no siren. He prayed no one would get in his way. The tires squealed as he turned right onto Main Street. Then he saw something up ahead. An accident was blocking the way out of town. He threw the car into reverse, and headed down the alley to work his way around. He knew his backup would be delayed, too.

Laurel lighted a candle, filled the tub with warm water and crawled in. Her body became soothed and so did her mind. She was satisfied that Claire's story had been revealed and now her spirit could rest.

Suddenly a thought flashed in Laurel's mind. Genevieve's son had not died. It was possible his descendants were still alive and here in Cedarville.

Then she heard it. There was a click at the front door. Someone was in the house. Laurel's breathing quickened and her pulse began to race. Horrified, she glanced toward the bathroom door. It was open! Should she make a lunge to lock it and run the risk of meeting the intruder face to face, or she should she remain quiet and hope he would not come down the hall? She chose the latter, for she could not bring herself to move.

Laurel stared down at her naked body. Its trembling was making ripples in the water. She could do nothing but wait for the inevitable.

She caught a movement in her peripheral vision. A man's hand reached around the corner and turned off the light. The flame of the candle flickered with the movement and Laurel saw a curl of smoke make its way toward the doorway. She closed her eyes for a second. When she opened them, Lucien Caulder stood above her. He was smiling. It was HER smile. "You're Genevieve's...."

"...Great grandson," Caulder finished her sentence.

"And it's Belle Rouge you've been after all this time."

Laurel started to get up, but Lucien pushed her back down. "I don't need either you or your daughter now. Someone bought my horse. It'll be enough for the down payment on Belle Rouge."

"I don't want to sell," Laurel said.

He grabbed her by the hair and pulled her to her feet. "You don't have to sell if you're dead."

Before Laurel could resist, he dragged her from the tub and pinned her to the floor with his knees. He opened a small flask. "Drink this." he demanded.

"One of Genevieve's recipes?" Laurel said as her teeth clamped down on his hand.

"You're going to pay for that," Lucien snarled. "Before you die, you're going to pay."

Laurel heard him unzip his pants. Vainly she tried to move her arms, but her strength was no match for his. "No!" She screamed. "You will not do this to me!"

Suddenly, she felt the weight of his body lift off her. She rolled out from under Lucien, and saw someone else's feet.

"You son of a bitch," John Miller yelled and slammed Lucien against the wall.

Caulder fell through the door and landed in the hall. In an instant, Miller was on top of him.

Laurel saw Lucien grapple for his pocket. "He's got a gun!" she screamed. But it was too late. The shot rang out.

John grimaced in agony and he bent sideways. With one last burst of energy, he grabbed Caulder's gun hand and slammed it against his knee. The gun slid toward Laurel's feet.

Lucien lunged at Miller, his hands closing around the deputy's neck.

"Stop it!" Laurel cried. "Lucien, stop!"

John Miller was gasping for breath. His life was being squeezed out of him.

Laurel picked up the gun and moved to where Caulder could see her. “I said stop. I’ll shoot!”

Lucien stood up over Miller’s limp body. “You don’t have the guts for it,” he smiled.

Laurel heard two pops as she blacked out.

# CHAPTER 21

Eva, Jane, John and Laurel came out of the courthouse into the bright and warm spring day.

Laurel took in a deep breath of fragrant air. "I'm glad that's over."

"So you thought you shot Lucien?" John laughed.

"I didn't see the sheriff standing there."

"But he saw plenty of you," Miller teased.

"That's not funny, John."

"It's all right, Jane," Laurel said. "I need something to make me laugh."

"We all do," Eva agreed.

John opened the car door. "Why don't the three of you go to Savannah now."

"I don't want to leave...," Laurel began.

"I'll be here when you get back. By that time, my divorce will be well on its way to being final."

"Just know one thing, John. I don't want to keep you away from the boy. I know you've raised him as if he were your son."

Miller kissed Laurel's cheek. "I love you for that," he said. "Go make your reservations. Tell cousin Marie hello for me."

"A bed and breakfast in Savannah sounds wonderful," Laurel said, "but I thought your cousin was elderly. How can she run a business?"

"Marie's quite active for her age. Besides, she has a partner in the business---a doctor----Julia something----. I can't recall her last name."

It was only a week later, when, by way of quiet narrow streets, the taxi wound around the small park-like squares in the historic district of Savannah, Georgia. A few yards from Chattam Square, the car stopped in front of a section of row houses. The fresh paint that adorned the doors of the two center dwellings set them apart from the others.

"Here we are ma'am," said the driver. "It's the house with the bright pink door."

A gracefully curved wrought-iron handrail led Laurel, Jane and Eva up the circular steps to the main entrance.

Suddenly, the heavy pink door opened and before them stood a short, slightly plump woman with an engaging smile. "I'm so sorry I couldn't meet you at the airport," she said, "but the cook's off today, and I had to prepare breakfast for my guests before I sent them off. Come in, come in! Driver, please take their luggage around back to the carriage house. I thought you might like it out there. It opens into the garden."

"That sounds wonderful, Marie," Jane smiled. I'd like you to meet my good friends, Eva Farnsworth and Laurel MacKenzie. Laurel, Eva, this is my cousin, Marie Buchanan."

"You have a beautiful home, Miss Buchanan," Eva returned her host's radiant smile.

"It's Marie. And thank you for the compliment. I turned the house into a bed and breakfast after I retired from teaching. I love meeting people."

"I hope we're not putting you out," Laurel interjected.

"Nonsense! For years I've wanted Jane to come. Let me show you to the carriage house."

Marie led them down the hallway of the narrow house, through the kitchen and onto a deck that spanned the length of the adjacent building.

"Do you own the house next door, too?" Laurel asked.

"Yes, Julia and I bought it together. We use this house for the bed and breakfast and the other as our residence. Julia lives on the second floor and I on the first. By the way, Julia's just dying to meet you, Miss MacKenzie. She's read all of your books."

Marie unlocked the door of the carriage house. "Julia and I have a very restful time planned for you. There are twin beds upstairs and this couch makes a bed. Admittedly though, the twin beds are more comfortable."

"This is great," Laurel said. "I don't mind the couch at all.

"I'm just so glad you're here," Marie smiled. "Julia will be home in about two hours, would you like to rest till then?"

Eva slumped into a well-worn chair. "I know I'd love to," she sighed.

"The five of us will eat together. You'll find Julia a little reserved, but, from what Jane told me, you and she have a lot in common, Laurel. Julia loves antiques and genealogy. She's traced her family back to New Orleans, Scotland and France. She's part Cajun, you know. But I should let her tell you. She probably won't volunteer anything about herself, though. You'll have to pry it out of her. Now, I'm off to fix supper. You rest."

After Marie closed the door, the three of them sat quietly for a moment, then simultaneously, they looked at one another and giggled. "Whew!" Eva exclaimed. "No wonder Julia is quiet, there's no time to get a word in when Marie's around."

"But she's such a dear," Jane said. "She's always been the mother hen where I'm concerned. I'm just sorry I didn't keep in touch these last few years."

"We're going to have a good time, I know that. But..."

"But what, Eva?" Laurel asked.

"I have a strange feeling we're here for some other reason, not just relaxation."

"Now wait," Jane stopped her. "All of that stuff is over. We've solved the mystery of Belle Rouge. Lucien Caulder's death ended it."

"No, there's more, and I think Julia may have something to do with it."

It was exactly two hours later when a soft rap came at the door. "Jane, ladies, are you up? Supper's ready."

"We'll be there in just a minute," Jane replied.

"Drat this watch!" Eva growled. "I can't seem to get it fastened."

"What's wrong with you?" Jane questioned. "Why are you so nervous?"

"I wish I knew."

"You aren't sorry you came, are you? You like Marie, don't you?"

"Who wouldn't like her, Jane? I told you I think we're supposed to be here. I just... Oh, I don't know what. I'm just silly. I'm probably just being silly."

Jane opened the door. "Let's go eat. You'll feel wonderful after you've eaten my cousin's cooking."

Eva followed Jane and Laurel up the stairs to the deck and into the dining room. She could see Marie in the kitchen, busily emptying the contents of various pots and pans into fine china bowls. But she sensed another presence even though she could see no one else.

"Sit down," Marie insisted. "Julia called. She's not going to be able to make it for supper. In fact, she's been called out of town. A patient of hers was visiting in Boston when she was taken ill. Of course, Julia would go to her. She doesn't know when she'll be back in town."

When the four women sat down at the sumptuous table, Marie asked Laurel to tell her what had happened at Belle Rouge. "Jane only whetted my appetite when she called."

Eva was aware of their voices, but her mind was on something else. She had to find a way into Julia's apartment.

When Laurel finished speaking, Marie said, "That's quite an intriguing story. "It was wise of you, Jane, to take Laurel away for a while. Her experience was very frightening. I don't know a thing about voodoo," Marie continued. "But Julia has made a study of it. You know it's still practiced by some of the people around New Orleans. And to think this Genevieve put a curse on all descendants of the Kilgores. But if she cursed all descendants of the Kilgores, and Lucien Caulder's great-grandmother was pregnant by Sumner Kilgore, then she unwittingly put a curse on her own son. Didn't you say Lucien was his descendent? Jane, that means your ba---."

"It's all right, Marie. They both know about my baby."

"That must be why I'm feeling so strange," Eva exclaimed. "Jane, your daughter could be in great danger. We have to find her."

"Marie, who adopted her?" Jane asked.

"Julia set it up. Only she would know."

The phone rang. It was John Miller. He asked for Jane. When she finished speaking she handed the phone to Laurel. Jane drew a deep breath. "John heard from a friend of his in Beaufort. He found out my child died as an infant."

"I'm so sorry," Marie consoled.

"I didn't know her, but I still feel she was a part of me," Jane said. "If you'll excuse me, I think I'd like to be alone for a while."

"You go on to the carriage house, dear. I'll entertain Eva and Laurel."

Laurel hung up the phone. "That has to be tough on her. I know she had hopes she'd meet her daughter some day."

"I don't know if Julia would have told her who adopted the child," Marie said, "but I believe she might have. She understands how both the mother and child would feel. If the adoptive parents had agreed, I think she would have arranged a meeting. Maybe Jane could still meet the parents---the couple."

"I don't know," Eva said. "Don't push it. Jane will tell you if she wants to do that."

Marie got up from the table. "Let me clear the dishes, and we'll go sit in the parlor."

"We'll help," Laurel offered.

By the time they had finished, Eva had hit on a plan to get into Julia's apartment. "Marie, do you think it would be possible for Laurel to see some of Julia's antiques? She's been talking about nothing else."

The surprise on Laurel's face dissipated when Eva poked her in the back. "Oh yes," she chimed in when she realized Eva had something up her sleeve. "I'd love to see them."

"I think we need to wait till Julia's here, but I'll show you my place. Julia decorated it with antiques, too."

Marie, Eva and Laurel walked across the deck and into the first floor apartment. "My bedroom is my favorite," Marie said. "Come look at it."

As they went through the parlor, Eva stopped at a desk. She picked up a framed photograph, then followed.

"It's a beautiful room," Laurel was saying. "Don't you love it, Eva?"

Eva did not answer the question, instead she held out the picture. "Who is this, Marie?" she asked.

"Dear God, that's Nila!" Laurel cried.

At Marie's insistence, Laurel related the story of the Cajun woman on the plane and the story of how she believed the same woman had saved her horse from being engaged in a catastrophe at the race track.

"It couldn't be my Julia," Marie laughed. "She hasn't been to Los Angeles or Kentucky lately. In fact, she's never been to Kentucky. She does have a medical conference coming up there shortly. She mentioned it would be her first trip to Kentucky."

It was late when Laurel and Eva got back to the carriage house. The lights were off, and they assumed Jane had fallen asleep upstairs.

Eva sat down on the couch. "I know she's Nila. That's what my strange feeling was the minute we got here. Julia and Nila are the same person."

"I know they are, too" Laurel responded. "Look at this. This piece of junk mail was in the trash basket beside the desk. It's addressed to Julia Nila -----." Laurel stopped.

"What is it?" Eva asked.

"Her last name is Castile. That's the name of the woman in my dream. You know, the one about my agent and the woman who was to produce and direct the movie."

"Well, I'll be damned," Eva said. "That's it and I missed it."

"Missed what?" Laurel asked.

"I was interpreting your dream incorrectly. It was not what happened in your dream that was important. It was those two words---produce and direct. Ms. Castile was producing and directing 'The Secrets of Cedarville'. Laurel, Julia's the one who generated everything that's been happening at Belle Rouge."

"But why her?" Laurel questioned again. "I thought it was Barney wanting to make sure all the truths were known."

"No," Eva said. "It's Dr. Castile. "We're not finished with this mystery yet."

At Marie's insistence they had busied themselves by touring the city and doing what any ordinary tourists would do, but Julia Castile had still not returned to Savannah when they were nearing the end of their visit.

Jane was in the main house with Marie on their last afternoon in Savannah, and Eva and Laurel were walking back from the Photo-Mat when Laurel asked a question. "Why didn't you wait until we got home to have the film developed?"

"I just wanted to see something," Eva answered.

"No, something else is going on in your head. What is it?"

Eva handed Laurel the photographs. "Take a look at these pictures, and tell me what you see."

"I see old houses, cars parked in front of them, Chattam Square and..."

"Let me put it another way. What's MISSING?"

"I don't know what you're driving at."

"There are no people in the photographs."

"Yes there are. In this one. See there in the distance, there's a person."

"That's you," Eva replied. You were standing on the steps of the Presbyterian church when I was trying to get a full shot of the steeple. You're wearing your yellow slacks and plaid shirt."

"You're right," Laurel laughed. "I guess I'm thinner than I was." She studied the pictures a little more. "I'd say the streets are deserted because Savannah's a quiet town. There were plenty of people around when we took the tour the other day."

"Yes, I know. Why aren't they in my pictures?"

They crossed the street and headed through Chattam Square. "Look," Laurel exclaimed. "Julia's gotten home."

"How do you know Dr. Castile's home?" Eva asked.

"There she is, standing in the window on the second floor."

Marie assured them Julia was not in the house. It must have been a shadow Laurel saw, and Marie said, once again, she was indeed sorry they would not get to meet Dr. Castile.

They finished packing their suitcases and at one o'clock on the dot, Marie called from the main house. "Jane! Laurel! Eva! The taxi's here!"

Laurel sat her luggage down in the front hallway and hugged Marie. "Thank you for having us. You don't know how much I needed this rest. When are you coming to visit us?"

"Oh, I don't leave town anymore. I'm getting too old to travel."

"Nonsense!" Laurel said. "Bring Julia, too. Or tell her to give me a call when she's in Louisville for the medical conference."

The driver picked up the luggage and put it in the trunk. Laurel climbed in the front seat, but Eva paused to watch as Jane turned to embrace Marie.

With a profound look of sadness on her face, Marie held tightly to Jane. "Till we meet again," she said.

As the taxi pulled away, Eva Farnsworth watched the lonely figure standing on the circular steps, silhouetted against the pink door of the row house.

"If you don't mind, ladies," the driver said, "we'll pick up another passenger at the hospital. She said it was urgent that she get to the airport. Thought you'd understand since she was a doctor."

"Do you know the doctor's name?" Eva asked.

"Castile, I believe she said."

"That's what I thought," Eva muttered.

The woman slid in the seat beside Eva. "What a coincidence, Dr. Castile, that you should pick this taxi."

"Yes. Isn't it. I did so want to meet you. I'm sorry I had to be out of town."

"Dr. Castile, was it you who placed my baby in the adoption?"

"Yes, Jane. They were a lovely couple. The baby died at six months---sudden infant death syndrome. They were heartbroken."

"You kept in contact with them?"

"Oh yes," the doctor replied.

"Speaking of contact...," Eva began.

Dr. Castile quickly changed the subject. "I've read your novels Ms. Mackenzie. I hear there's another one in the works about your new home, Belle Rouge."

"How did you know?"

"How do you think?" Eva muttered.

"Why are you going to the airport, Doctor, instead of going home?" Jane asked.

"I'm due at the conference in two days. I saw no reason to go home first. I called Marie just after you left. She knows what I'm doing."

"I wish I did," Eva said.

"Looks like it might rain, ladies." The driver broke in.

Julia's tall frame bent down to study the sky through the window of the car. "We won't take this flight if it storms."

"Where you ladies headed?"

"To Louisville," Eva answered.

"By way of Charlotte?"

"Yes sir." This time it was Laurel who spoke.

"We're on the edge of the storm here, but it's heading that way. It's due to hit Charlotte about the time you arrive, but they won't let the plane take off in a storm."

"They have before," came Julia's reply.

John Miller was sitting at the airport waiting for the arrival of Jane, Eva and Laurel when he heard his named being paged.

"Would Mr. John Miller please pick up the white telephone for a message. Mr. Miller for a message."

John felt his stomach tighten. "Oh God, something's happened."

He picked up the phone, said his name and listened. Then he released a big sigh as he plopped himself down on a nearby chair. They were in Charlotte and it was storming. Dr. Castile was coming home with them and had insisted they wait for the next flight.

The rain was pelting against the windows of the terminal in Charlotte. Dr. Castile had chosen to sit apart from them. Eva watched the strange woman as she stared toward the blackened sky.

"I was a little embarrassed at the way Julia treated that airline clerk," Jane whispered.

"She was just firm," Laurel answered. "But I am beginning to think you're right, Eva. There is something more than a little odd about her."

"Yes," Eva quipped. "There is something a bit odd about a woman who appears in airplanes and hands someone a poem. There's a little something odd when the same woman shows up at a racetrack and saves a horse."

"That's not the person who pushed me down the stairs," Jane said.

"Of course it isn't," Eva shot back. "That had to be Genevieve. This woman is here to protect."

"She certainly is strange," Jane said.

"No. I think she's DRIVEN", Eva replied. "It's as if she has a plan she's carrying out, but I haven't figured out what it is."

"I'm sure you will. I'm going to get something to drink, do you want anything?" Laurel asked.

"No thanks. You both go ahead."

For a few more moments, Eva Farnsworth studied Julia Nila Castile, whose gaze had turned from the sky to the runway. She walked toward the doctor and sat down beside her. "Can you tell me what's troubling you?" she asked the brooding figure.

"I couldn't let you get on that flight."

"I know, Julia. That's why I took your side in the argument with the clerk."

"I didn't want to be rude. But I knew there were seats on the later flight. She just didn't want to do the paper work."

"I understand. You owe me no explanation. Except..."

"You want to know why," Julia finished her sentence.

"Yes, I do. I need to know so I can help you."

Julia Castile's eyes turned toward Eva. The intense pain they conveyed forced Eva to wince. "Julia," she pleaded. "Tell me what I need to know."

"The secrets are found close to home," came the reply.

Final call: Flight 636 to Louisville now departing at gate 6."

Julia Castile resumed her anxious vigil.

John Miller felt a great deal of relief when he learned they were waiting out the storm, but there was still something bothering him. He was too restless to sit any three hours waiting for the arrival of their rescheduled flight.

He had been keeping a watch on Belle Rouge for Laurel, but he decided he would use the time to drive down and take one more look around before she got home.

Nothing seemed out of the ordinary when he turned in the drive. He would check inside the house. He pulled the key Laurel had given him out of his pocket and opened the door.

The house was quiet. He walked down the hallway toward the bathroom. None of the blood stains remained. He was happy to see the ordeal Laurel experienced there didn't seem to bother her as much as he thought it might. Then too, he knew how much she loved Belle Rouge. It would take more than Lucien Caulder's death to make her want to leave.

Nothing seemed out of order. Then for some reason he looked out the side window. He saw it. An old dilapidated truck sat at the back of the small barn.

"You sure you don't want something to drink?" Laurel asked.

Eva Farnsworth shook her head.

"How about you, Julia, would you like...? What's going on with you two?"

Before an answer came, Julia Castile gripped the arms of her seat, pulling herself forward. Eva, Jane and Laurel followed her horrified stare just in time to see Flight 636 gather speed for it's take off. The plane's wheels had barely risen above the ground when a terrific bolt of lightening split the sky. Suddenly the plane lost power and plummeted to the earth.

Round and round the plane careened on the rain-slick runway. Then it tilted to the right, shearing off one wing. As if in slow motion, it flipped over. Bright orange exploded from one of the engines and quickly enveloped the body of the plane.

"God help them," Eva whispered.

"That could have been us!" Laurel cried. "If Julia hadn't..."

Quietly, John Miller opened the door of the barn. He was greeted by a damp musty odor. He waited for his eyes to adjust to the darkness.

Just then, the back door opened and a figure darted out of the barn. John attempted to follow, but he was slowed by the wood that had been stored in the runway.

When he reached the open door, he saw a small black man slide behind the wheel of the truck. Just as the motor started, the man turned to look at John. His face was horribly disfigured.

John didn't attempt to follow the truck. He knew who it was, and he knew why Barney had now appeared to him. He was in love with Laurel and Barney now trusted him. And John knew Barney was here at Belle Rouge at this particular time for a reason. The reason was evident. There was something in the barn the black man wanted him to find.

The building was mostly filled with lumber and tools, nothing of importance. When John opened the door to what appeared to be a special storage room, he knew he had found what Barney had wanted. A lone marble-top dresser sat in the corner of the room. A key was protruding from one of the drawers.

He turned the key and the lock clicked. Slowly he pulled the drawer open. Inside was a book. He retrieved it and went outside into the light.

As he was about to open the book, he glanced at his watch. He barely had time to make it back to the airport. He jumped in his car, turned it around and headed out the drive.

"Why in the world would Barney want me to find a Bible?" he asked himself.

# CHAPTER 22

Laurel was first off the plane. She saw John coming toward them. "Here, over here!" she waved. "Oh John, am I ever glad to see you! Did you hear about the crash? If Julia hadn't insisted, we would have been on that flight!"

"No, I left, so I didn't hear anything. You mean your original flight crashed?"

"On take off. And it's because of Julia that we weren't on it."

Julia was the last to leave the plane. John recognized her immediately as the woman Laurel had described as a passenger on her flight from L.A. From the look on Eva's face, he decided not to bring up the subject. Instead, he held out his hand. The feel of the doctor's hand was cold and clammy.

"I want to thank you," he said. "for insisting on the later flight."

"I'm glad I could be there," came the soft reply.

Laurel led the way toward the main terminal. Dr. Castile walked beside her, with Jane just in back of them. Eva fell in beside John, some distance behind.

"What's going on?" he asked.

"No time to explain," Eva said. "Let's you and me make a stop at the airline desk."

"You know something. Don't you?" John persisted.

"Just listen," she said as she smiled at the clerk.

"May I help you?" the young lady greeted them.

"Yes," Eva studied the arrival board. "I notice you have the five o'clock flight from Charlotte arriving on time."

"Yes ma'am. In fact, it arrived a few minutes ahead of schedule. Were you supposed to meet someone?"

"A Dr. Julia Nila Castile. Would you check to see if she was on it?"

The clerk ran her pencil down the list. "I'm sorry. She wasn't booked on that flight. Maybe she was on the nine thirty one."

"I don't think so," Eva smiled. "By the way, was there any trouble on the five o'clock flight?"

The smile faded from the clerk's face. "No. Not this time."

"What do you mean?" John asked.

The clerk lowered her eyes. "That flight crashed a year ago today. You may have read about it. A bolt of lightening struck the plane on takeoff at Charlotte. One of the flight attendants was a good friend. I hated to lose her."

Eva reached out and took the girl's hand. "My dear, I doubt that we can ever lose a friendship. It stays with us forever."

Laurel lifted a briefcase from the luggage carousel. On it was printed, Dr. J. N. Castile. "Julia, I don't remember you having that briefcase when we left."

"Oh, I decided to let it go with the baggage and not carry it on board. I'm glad you found it. It contains some very important information, and, for a moment, I was afraid it might have been lost with the transfer in Charlotte."

"No, it's here and safe," Laurel replied. She glanced over her shoulder. "Where are Eva and John."

"There they come, down the escalator," Jane answered.

They followed the sky cap out the door. "Julia's here for a conference at Jewish Hospital, John," Laurel said, "but she's going to spend the night at Belle Rouge first."

"Mr. Miller," Julia tugged at John's arm to hold him back. "This is a very important briefcase. Do you understand?"

"Yes, I understand."

When they turned into Belle Rouge, John spoke. "I almost forgot. I found this Bible in a dresser in the small barn today."

"There's a dresser in the barn?" Laurel asked. "I never saw it."

"I think it may have just arrived."

"But who brought it?"

"I saw Barney, Laurel. He's what drew me to the barn."

"Thank God someone else has seen him besides me," Laurel said. "I thought I might be hallucinating."

John stopped the car in the circular driveway. "You never mentioned his disfigurement before."

"He isn't disfigured."

"Yes, he is," John said. "It looked like a burn."

"Of course," Laurel said. "He tried to save Belle Rouge when it caught on fire. He must have been burned then. I only wish I knew what became of him. I wonder if he went to England with Bruce MacCallum? Wait a minute! MacCallum. Eva, wasn't that the name of the apprentice jockey Allen Williams said he was going to put on Lion the next time he ran?"

"It sure was," Eva answered. "I never put the two names together."

"I have got to talk to him," Laurel said.

"He's in town," John replied. "I saw him at the training center, just yesterday."

"Good. He has to be a relative of Bruce and Alexandra," Laurel said. "It's not late. Can everyone come in? Let's see what we need to find in this Bible?"

John held the front door open for them. "Your mail's on the table there," he said.

Laurel quickly picked up one envelope and tore into it. “This is wonderful,” she said. “Beth will be here in the morning. I wrote and told her about Lucien. She still insists I not pick her up. She’ll get a taxi.”

Laurel glanced back at the doorway where Julia was standing. “Come in,” she said. “No need to hesitate.”

Julia studied the grand staircase. “The house, it’s just so beautiful.”

“Let’s go into the kitchen,” Laurel suggested. “We can sit around the table and look at the Bible.”

When they were all seated, she opened the book. “I knew it. This is the Kilgore family Bible. The genealogy is on the first page.”

Laurel slid the book toward Eva. “You’re more versed in genealogies than I am. Study it and see what you make of it.”

“There’s a list of all the family names.”

“Read them out loud,” Julia urged.

Eva began, “Do you recognize the handwriting, Laurel?”

“Yes. It’s Lily’s.”

Eva continued. “Here’s Sumner’s date of birth, here’s Lily’s, Ross’, two miscarriages and then Claire’s birth.”

“Are the dates of their deaths written in?” John asked.

“Yes. And it had to be Claire who did it.”

“Not her own death,” Laurel interjected. “Is the date of her death recorded?”

“It’s here. Two years after Sumner died.”

“Oh, good lord!” Eva exclaimed.

“What is it?” Laurel asked.

“Someone has printed in the name of Claire’s child! I’d know that handwriting anywhere. It’s Barney’s.”

“What could have happened to the child?” Jane questioned. “And why did Barney write in the name? Why didn’t Claire?”

It was Julia who spoke. "There are other unsolved parts to this mystery. You may want to look closer at the Bible."

"I hadn't noticed this," Eva said. "Here are some old newspaper clippings stuck between these pages."

"Read them. They must be important," Laurel encouraged her.

"I'd say they are! It's the account of how Sumner died."

"How, Eva? How?" Laurel asked impatiently.

"His body was found in the burned-out remains of the kitchen wing at Belle Rouge. A female servant named Genevieve died with him. The black jockey named Barnabas was badly burned trying to rescue them. Your writing was correct, Laurel. You were right on the mark."

"Only Claire and Barnabas were left at Belle Rouge," Laurel sighed. "But Claire lived only two more years. What happened to the baby? Did Barnabas raise her?"

"No black man would have been allowed to care for a white child," John said. "Maybe some of their friends..."

"Claire had only two other friends, besides Barnabas," Eva interrupted. "Dr. James and Alexandra Lennox, and Dr. James was already dead."

"What could have become of the baby?" Jane asked, her voice filled with sadness.

"In time, Jane," Julia responded.

Eva searched the Bible for more clippings. "There's nothing in here to indicate Claire was ever questioned about the deaths."

"No, I don't think she would be," John added. "If Preston Miller had any suspicions that Claire had anything to do with it, I think he would have taken Barnabas' word that Genevieve killed Sumner."

"And the fire?" Eva asked.

"If something caught on fire during the struggle, it would have spread fast, but because the kitchen was off in a wing at the back, there was time for the neighbors to get there to save the rest of the house."

Julia smiled. "That's logical, John."

Eva turned toward Dr. Castile. "We're not finished, are we? There's one final piece in the puzzle. Isn't there?"

"I feel there is," Julia smiled again.

# CHAPTER 23

Laurel convinced everyone to spend the night at Belle Rouge because of the lateness of the hour. She knew they all needed to be there the next morning to put the final piece of the puzzle together.

Though she had slept relatively well, Laurel remembered waking up periodically during the night. Something was trying to come through to her from her subconscious. Now as she lay, half awake, she could almost recall what it was. When she heard Eva call her name, she lost all train of thought.

"Laurel! Beth's here."

She jumped out of bed and hastily put on a robe. Beth was waiting for her in the front hallway. "Boy, Mom. It must have been some party with all these people left over," she grinned.

Laurel hugged her daughter. "I'm so happy you're here, but there was no party. This morning we're here to finish the mystery of Belle Rouge."

"You finished your book?" Beth asked.

"Almost, just the final chapter to go. I'm talking about the REAL mystery concerning this farm. You're just in time to hear all our findings."

Everyone gathered in the kitchen---Laurel, Eva, Jane, John and Beth. Dr. Julia Castile had disappeared.

"I really wanted Beth to meet Julia," Laurel said. "I can't believe she left without even saying good-bye. I'm going to call the medical conference and have them page her. I'd feel better knowing she got there safely. Besides, she left her briefcase. I'll get the phone book."

"No...." John rose to stop her.

"I'm sure she needs the briefcase."

"Let her go," Eva whispered. She'll have to know about Julia sooner or later."

"Here we are." Laurel sat back down at the table and reached for the phone. "It'll just take a minute."

"Hello. .... Yes, I'm sure you can help me. Would you please get a message to Dr. Julia Castile. She's attending the conference there. .... But you must be mistaken. I'm sure she said Jewish Hospital. .... That doesn't make sense. .... The conference was last year? .... I don't understand. --- Well, I'm sure you know. Good-bye."

Laurel hung up the receiver. "That's strange. Maybe Julia was mistaken about the date and flew back to Savannah."

She picked up the receiver once again. "Jane, will you call Marie and find out if she knows anything. I can see how Julia could have the wrong week, but the wrong year? That's incredible. May I get on the extension while you call?"

Laurel went into the study and picked up the phone just as a recorded voice came on the line.

"That number has been changed to 555-1642."

Laurel waited patiently while Jane dialed the new number. "Hello," came the voice on the other end of the line.

"Marie?"

"No. This is her nurse."

"Nurse?" Jane questioned. "Is my cousin sick?"

Your cousin?"

"I'm Jane Miller. Marie's my cousin. What's going on?"

"Oh, I'm sorry, Miss Miller, I didn't know to call you. Marie has suffered a stroke."

"When? I just saw her yesterday."

"You couldn't have, Miss Miller. No one's been here."

"Yes, I was there. Two of my friends and I just visited Marie and stayed at her bed and breakfast."

"There's some kind of a mistake. Marie hasn't lived at the bed and breakfast for about a year."

"Who are you?" Jane demanded.

"I used to be Dr. Castile's office nurse, but now I tend to Marie since she's had a stroke."

"Is Dr. Castile there?"

"Is this some kind of a joke?"

"No, I assure you. Please tell me about Marie's stroke."

"Well, let's see. It was June 14. Why, that was yesterday! Yes, it was a year ago yesterday. Dr. Castile left at about five in the afternoon on the 14th to fly to a medical conference in Louisville. According to the cook, Marie had a headache that afternoon, and she went to bed as soon as Dr. Castile left. She didn't have the radio or TV on, so she didn't hear about it. Oh, it was tragic, Miss Miller, the way she got the news."

"What news?"

"The news about Dr. Castile, of course. She and Marie were like sisters."

"Please go on," Jane urged.

"A man came to the door the next morning with Julia's luggage, everything except her briefcase. The airline had lost it. He told Marie how sorry he was about Julia's plane. Her luggage had been left at the Charlotte airport, so it wasn't aboard Flight 636 when it crashed. The man who delivered the luggage said Marie was standing there in front of the pink door when he left. He must not have seen her fall. The cook found her on the stoop. Then she phoned me."

"Miss Miller, we moved out here in the suburbs as soon as Marie was released from the hospital. We haven't been able to sell the two row houses. Some of the neighbors got some silly story started about how they see Dr. Castile's ghost standing in the second floor window. No one will buy the houses when they hear that story. Miss Miller? Miss Miller, are you there?"

"Yes. I'm here. What's Marie's condition?"

"At one time, she was able to say a few words I could understand. But for the last two days she's just been repeating Dr. Castile's name. I'm afraid it won't be long now. Shall I notify you when the end comes?"

"Yes, please do. Will you give her my love?"

"Of course I will. But I'm not sure she understands anything I say to her."

Jane's voice was hardly audible. "I think she does. Here's my number....please call me."

Laurel hung up and rushed to the kitchen.

"Did you hear all of it?" Jane asked her.

"Yes, I did," Laurel said. "This has something to do with the way you were feeling in Savannah. Doesn't it, Eva?"

"Yes, it does."

"When we flew there, I believe we were transported back in time to a year ago," Eva began.

"A la 'Star Trek'?" Beth interjected.

"Something like that. Some people say time is relative and concurrent, just on different levels."

"That's as good a description as we can get," John agreed.

"What you're talking about is beyond me," Beth smiled. "Mom phoned me just before the Savannah trip and told me everything that had happened since she moved to Cedarville. It's an amazing story."

"The most amazing thing is the fact that Jane and John are descendants of Sheriff Miller and Eva is a descendant of the Doctor who was killed. And the strangest of all was that Lucien Caulder was a descendant of Genevieve. He tried to destroy us to get Belle Rouge, just as Gen destroyed the Kilgores," Laurel noted.

"He was an evil person," Beth said. "I despise him for what he did to us, but I can't believe he'd stoop to trying to murder you."

"He knew you'd never want the farm if I was dead. He had scraped together the money to buy it."

"I may not have sold it. I would have tried to keep Belle Rouge because of what it means to you."

Laurel felt the tears well up in her eyes. "Thank you Beth, you don't know what it means to hear you say that."

"But, may I ask a question? Eva once told me she descended from Dr. James through his youngest son who came back here to live. Jane how do you and John descend from Sheriff Miller?"

"Sheriff Miller married later in life and they had two sons. The eldest was my father---the youngest was John's. Preston was killed on duty a few months after John's father was born."

"Who by?" Beth asked.

"The murder went unsolved," Jane answered.

"But there were rumors," John said. "By God!" he slapped his knee. "There was talk that a young man who lived down by the river ambushed him. He was a mulatto. I'd bet anything it was Genevieve's son. The young man disappeared after the shooting. Some ten years later Lucien's relatives moved into the house."

"And what of Barnabas and Alexandra?" Beth asked.

"The last we know, they both went to England," Laurel responded. "We suspect the English jockey Allen Williams is going to use is a relative."

"That's where we are, Beth," Eva sighed. "But I still feel there's something else we don't know. Julia came to us this final time for some reason. What was it? What did she want us to...."

"Wait a minute," John interrupted. "She said something to me at the airport. She said I should remember that her briefcase is important. That's why Julia came back with you---to make sure you got the briefcase."

"But why was Julia so involved?" Jane asked.

John opened the briefcase. "I think we're about to find out."

# CHAPTER 24

A handwritten letter lay on top of the papers in Julia's briefcase. "Read it out loud," Laurel urged John.

*Dear Ms. Mackenzie,*

*May I first say that I have read, with a great deal of interest, all of your books. At this moment, I am sitting in the Charlotte airport waiting for my flight to depart. I picked up the local paper and read that you are in town for a speaking engagement this evening.*

"My gosh, I was in Charlotte at that time for a seminar," Laurel interjected. "Please read on, John."

*I have tried to persuade the ticket clerk to switch me to the nine thirty flight, but to no avail. If she had cooperated, I could have attended your speech and given you some information that I believe would interest you.*

*Since I cannot attend, I will mail the information to you when I arrive in Louisville. I must close now if I am to have time to check my luggage.*

*Sincerely,*
*Dr. Julia Nila Castile*

*P.S. Please read these documents in the order in which I have placed them in the envelopes. They will be more understandable that way.*

"It's rather frightening," Eva stated, "to know that we have finally arrived at the point of solving this mystery."

"Yes," Jane agreed, "it's taken a lot of endurance for all of us to get through this ordeal, but I am thankful for the experience. It's meant a lot to me to have some closure to a part of my life."

"I'd like to echo that," John said as he kissed Laurel on the cheek. "I feel we are all beginning a new part of our lives."

"You know I will," she said, kissing him on the cheek.

Jane took out a handkerchief. "Before we all start to cry will you please read what Julia wrote. I'm dying to know what's in there."

John opened the first of the manila envelopes. "Here's a note clipped to the first paper," he said.

*Ms. Mackenzie, this envelope will explain to you who I am. I knew it was you who I needed to contact when I heard you say, during an interview on TV, that you were thinking of moving back to your roots near Cedarville, Kentucky.*

John removed the note and set it aside, revealing the first paper. "It's Dr. Castile's genealogy." He then scanned the paper. "Well, I'll be damned!" he said.

"What is it? Tell us!" Laurel demanded.

John placed the genealogy on the table where everyone could see it.

Eva stared in disbelief. "Look who her great-grandmother is: Alexandra Lennox."

"Next paper," said John. "It's another note."

*My great-grandmother, Alexandra, never forgave herself for bringing Philippe Dumont into Claire Kilgore's life. She knew that Dr. James was Claire's father and that Sumner was the father of Claire's baby. When Dr. James told her his life was in danger, he gave Alexandra one page of his record book that he had purposely cut out, for it contained some very important information.*

"John, please look to see if that page is in the envelope."

"No, Laurel. Doctor Castile said to take the papers in order, and I'm going to. Now, back to the note."

*Alexandra knew that it had to be Gen who reported the details of Claire's visit in Louisville. That's how Sumner Kilgore had time to investigate Philippe.*

*Alexandra, till her dying day, held herself responsible for Claire's illness. She carefully documented everything that happened. Each generation of her family has been instructed to keep the papers, with the hope of one day correcting the wrongs she felt had been done.*

*It was not until my grandfather, who dedicated his life to the study of various religions of the Caribbean region, read these documents that anyone ever realized Gen had probably used voodoo to cause Claire's illness.*

*Voodoo was a common practice. Usually, some form of an animal or bird was made and placed inside a pillow to cast a spell on a person who slept with it.*

"That verifies what we suspected about that thing I found in my bedroom," Laurel said. "Lucien was trying to use some of Genevieve's voodoo on me."

"Is that the same bird-like thing that scared Lucien the day he sent me home," Beth asked.

"The same thing," Jane said. "I put it in his house to use some of his same medicine on him."

"What ever happened to it?" Laurel asked.

"I don't know," John answered. "I suppose Lucien did something with it. We'll probably never know."

Eva frowned. "Just like we still don't know how Jane fell down the stairs. She thinks someone pushed her, Beth."

"It was probably just my own clumsiness," Jane said.

"Please go on with Julia's writing," Laurel urged.

John began again.

*If you will proceed to the next envelope, you will see that I have been able to find out what happened to some of the other people connected to the story. Dr. James' wife and family never returned to Kentucky, with the exception of one of his sons. You may find that some of his relatives still live there.*

"That's me," Eva nodded.

*I am sure at least one of Preston Miller's relatives must still live in Cedarville.*

"There are two of us," John said, winking at Jane. He continued.

*Shortly after Claire died, Alexandra went back to Scotland, where her people originated and her husband was buried. Her daughter, my grandmother, was already married and living in New Orleans, and truthfully, Alexandra and her son-in-law were never friendly. You see, he was Cajun and she was never able to overcome her prejudice toward him.*

*When Alexandra returned to Scotland, she took Barnabas with her, gave him the last name of MacCallum, her maiden name, and established him as a trainer of the Thoroughbred stock she purchased and put on the ancestral estate. He remarried and had two children, Claire and William. I will be going to Scotland next year to see if I can find any of his kin. I believe one of his great-grandchildren settled in Sussex, England and followed in the horse business.*

"The jockey at the training center isn't Alexandra's descendant. He's Barney's. I can't wait to talk with him. Can you believe it? A relative of Barnabas will be riding for me," Laurel smiled. "Is that all of the writings?"

"No," John said. "There's one more envelope."

When the envelope was opened, Julia Castile's final letter was revealed.

*Ms. Mackenzie, I'm sure you're wondering why the Kilgore family and all their secrets should descend upon you and not the other residents who have lived at Belle Rouge. Not only have I tried to fulfill Alexandra's desire to right the wrongs she felt she had done, but I have also had the burning desire to know what happened to Claire's child. I knew, if I didn't do it, no one would, for I am the last of Alexandra's kin.*

*Ms. Mackenzie, last month I completed my task. Enclosed is the page of Dr. James' record book, which he cut out and gave to Alexandra. He cut that information out for fear of what prejudice might follow the child. He wanted the youngster to have a fresh start in life.*

*Claire had a little girl. In the time following Sumner's death, when Claire became increasingly ill, Barnabas did his best to help raise the baby. But both he and Alexandra grew fearful that Claire might harm the baby when she was in one of her fits of depression. Together, they made the decision to take the little girl away from Claire. Preston Miller knew a local family planning to move back to North Carolina. They took Claire Kilgore's daughter, Lily Dee, with them and adopted her. It was a terrible decision with which both Barnabas and Alexandra had to live. I believe one reason Alexandra moved to Scotland was that she was afraid she might have second thoughts and try to find the baby. She knew the baby was in a marvelous home, and she knew she should never take her away from the adoptive family.*

*Claire signed the papers during one of her lucid moments. She, too, knew it was the best thing. She signed with one stipulation, that the little girl's given name had to remain Lily Dee.*

"Dr. Castile has certainly done her research," Jane said.

"Yes," Eva agreed. "It fills in a lot of gaps for us."

"Mom, what's wrong, Mom?" Beth asked.

"Don't anyone say any more till I get back. I'll just be a minute."

"Do you know what's going on?" John asked.

"No," Eva replied. "I have no idea."

In a few seconds, Laurel returned, a piece of paper in her hand. "Go ahead and read the rest of Julia's information."

*Ms. Mackenzie, I have written, in the form of a genealogy, Lily Dee's adoptive family's lineage, up to the current time. God bless you and your family, Ms. Mackenzie. I believe mine now rests in peace.*

*Till we meet again*
*Julia N. Castile*
*Exodus 18:2*

"I wonder why Dr. Castile found it necessary to give us Lily Dee's genealogy," John asked as he lifted the folded paper from the briefcase.

"I think..."

The ringing of the telephone interrupted Laurel's statement. "I'll get it. Hello. .... Oh yes, she's here." Laurel handed the phone to Jane. "This call's been forwarded from your number."

"Yes," Jane answered. ---- "When did she die?" ---- "You mean just a few minutes ago?" ---- "That's amazing." ----

"Yes, please call me again as soon as the arrangements have been made. I'll be there for the funeral." Jane hung up the phone.

"I'm sorry," Eva consoled her, but this is so amazing. Jane, do you remember what Marie said to you just before you got in the taxi?"

"Yes, I do. She said 'til we meet again', the same thing Julia wrote to close her letter."

"The circle is complete," Eva spoke softly.

"Not quite," Laurel said as she unfolded the paper she had brought into the room. She placed it beside Lily Dee's genealogy. "I think if you look closely, you'll find these two papers have some similarities."

"What is this?" John questioned.

"It's my family's genealogy," Laurel said.

"Dear God in heaven," John sighed. "Lily Dee's name is on both of them. Lily Dee was---."

"My grandmother," Laurel finished his sentence. "When Julia wrote about the family adopting the child and moving to North Carolina, I knew she was talking about my grandmother. The picture I have of the Prices standing in front of their store in Cedarville---that's the couple who adopted Claire's child."

The room was hushed till Eva spoke. "No wonder Gen's fetish affected you---you're Sumner Kilgore's great-great-granddaughter. Her curse was against the Kilgore family, not just Claire. Thank the Lord, we continued to search for answers."

"I can't believe it," Laurel shook her head. "Let me get this straight---Claire, my great-grandmother, was the result of an affair her mother had with Dr. James. Claire's baby was fathered by Sumner Kilgore."

"Wait!" Eva yelled. "Has anyone realized what else this means?" Before an answer came, she continued. "Laurel and I share something more than friendship. We share a common relative, Dr. Timothy James. We're family!"

"God bless Dr. Castile," Jane sighed.

"Yes indeed," John smiled. "God bless her."

"We're ignoring something," Beth said. "Didn't Dr. Castile write the number of a Bible verse at the end of her letter?"

"Yes, she did," John answered. "Eva...why don't you look it up? The Kilgore Bible is still here on the table."

"It's already open to Exodus 18," Eva exclaimed. "The newspaper articles we read last night mark the chapter."

"Read it, please," said Laurel.

Eva began.

*If thou shalt do this thing, and God command thee so, then thou shalt be able to endure, and all this people shall also go to their rest in peace.*

"It's all over," Eva sighed as she closed the book.

"But the curse," Beth said, "If it were placed on the Kilgores, and Mom and I are related to them, isn't it still in effect?"

Eva pondered the question for a moment. Then she answered, "I don't think so. I think the curse would be broken with the death of the last of Genevieve's descendants, and that happened when Lucien died."

Suddenly, Beth rose from the table.

"What is it?" Laurel asked. "You're so pale. Are you ill?"

"Just a bit queasy. I guess it was the flight and all the excitement. I'll think I'll lie down in your room, Mom."

"Do you want me to come with you?" Laurel asked.

"I just need to rest. That's all. You stay here."

Beth walked down the hallway toward Laurel's room. The nausea was so intense, she fell onto the bed and closed her eyes. When the attack subsided, she opened her eyes and there on the pillow opposite her was the fetish of the bird.

A pain in her stomach wrenched her double. Lucien Caulder's baby was moving inside her.

www.ingramcontent.com/pod-product-compliance
Lightning Source LLC
Chambersburg PA
CBHW060633260626
47161CB00008B/2878

* 9 7 8 1 9 3 8 2 3 0 7 3 8 *